TRAITOR

ALSO BY THE AUTHOR:

Military Men Series:

Hostile
Private
Traitor

Other Books:

Tied Down

TRAITOR

MILITARY MEN BOOK THREE

Leila Haven

ISBN: 1530998379
ISBN-13: 978-1530998371

DEDICATED TO ALL THOSE THAT LOVE
A BAD BOY.

CHAPTER ONE

JENNIFER

The flight was cancelled. *Cancelled.* I was left to bide my time at the airport indefinitely. A line was already forming at the check-in counter – a whole plane worth of people trying to get some answers.

If I didn't turn up to work on time my boss was going to have a heart attack. It wasn't like I could just get another connecting flight, they weren't frequent enough where I was going.

I finally made it to the front of the queue. "Ma'am, the earliest flight we can arrange will be arriving at approximately ten o'clock."

That was four hours away.

"Do you want me to book you in?" The perfectly dressed woman looked at me, her fingers poised over the keyboard.

It wasn't like I really had a choice. I needed to get there as fast as possible and driving would take much longer than the plane.

"Fine, yes, please. Book me in."

I was given a new boarding pass before I left the gate. There wasn't much else to do in the airport except eat so I headed for the bar.

"Your best house red, please," I ordered from the bartender. He nodded and poured me a glass, leaving me to stare into it for the next four hours.

I swiveled around on the stool and had a look around the lounge. It was largely empty, only passengers from my cancelled flight seemed to be lingering. They were a mixture of people, from elderly couples to businesspeople ready to relax for a while.

One guy caught my eye and made me stop. He was looking directly at me. I watched as he raised his beer in a 'cheers' gesture. I held up my glass in response.

There was a sparkle to the man's eyes, one that I bet got him into a lot of trouble all the time. His body was buff, I could see the bulges of muscles underneath his tight black T-shirt. His jeans hugged his hips in all the right ways.

It was too dark to see the color of his eyes but I would have put good money on the fact they were blue. With his short sandy blond hair, he looked like an all-American hunk.

I had to tear my gaze away as my cheeks burned hot. While I was looking at him all the thoughts in my head had turned dirty and wild. I wasn't normally so turned on by a guy just for holding my gaze but I could practically feel the sparks from across the room.

My first glass of wine was quickly finished. The bartender was busy with some other patrons so I was left to stare into my empty glass. A cancelled flight and empty wine glass, my night couldn't get any worse.

"Airports suck," a voice appeared at my side, startling me. I hadn't heard anyone take the next stool beside me.

I didn't need to lift my gaze to know it was the man I'd been fucking in my head. I looked anyway, curious to see him up close. I was wrong about his eyes, they were chocolate brown.

A warm, gooey chocolate brown.

"I take it you're trying to get to Los Angeles, too?" I said. He took a long gulp of his beer before he replied.

"Trying to. Not really succeeding so far." He had a chuckle to his voice that gave me goosebumps. I wanted to kiss those sexy lips until I tasted his laughter.

"I'm trying to get to my next work assignment."

"I'm heading back to work," he said. "A buddy of mine just got married."

The bartender finally topped up my glass. I clinked it on the guy's beer bottle. "Congratulations to your buddy and his Mrs."

We both took a gulp and laughed. The wine was going straight to my head, making me more courageous than I normally was. Heat was being generated between us and I'd barely said a word to him.

"I'm stuck here for another four hours," he said. "How about you?"

"Same. Four long hours in a boring airport. What's a girl to do?"

"I can think of plenty of things you could do."

My eyebrows rose in question. The wine was definitely making me feel all warm and tingly. Either that or it was the gorgeous Adonis at my side. "Really? And what would those plenty of things be?"

"You could go shopping."

"The stores are all closed."

"You could keep drinking."

"I'm already feeling a buzz," I challenged. The way he was looking at me made my stomach do backflips. I wanted to pour wine down his chest and lick it off his warm skin.

"You could read."

"My Kindle is in my checked luggage."

He held a napkin between his fingers. "You could tear this up and see how long a strip you could make. I hear there's a world record."

"I wouldn't want to take someone's world record

away from them. Plus, they might disqualify me for being slightly-drunk."

He pretended to think really hard. "You are making this difficult, you know that?"

I couldn't suppress the laughter playing on my lips. "Maybe you should think outside the box."

The guy put down his drink and leaned in closer, so close I could feel his breath tickling my neck and sending a shiver down my spine. "You could let me lead you into a private corner where I can rip all your clothes off. Then I would bend you over and fuck you until your mind is senseless from the pleasure."

My body was officially on fire. He didn't need to do anything to scramble my brain because it already was. My breathing was ragged, hitching in my throat and making my pulse race.

He leaned backwards and his gaze went straight back to his beer, like he hadn't just whispered filthy words in my ear.

It was impossible to tear my eyes away from him. I watched as he drank from his bottle and finished off his beer. I saw his Adam's apple bob when he swallowed. Then I was jealous of his bottle as his strong hands wrapped around it.

I was speechless. No man had ever given me such an indecent proposal before and I was *actually considering it.* There was a raw sexual attraction between us that had nothing to do with personality or common interests. I wanted his naked body wrapped around mine, I wanted his cock to fill me, and I wanted it right now.

"Okay," I said, almost in a whisper while I tried to find my voice again.

"You sure about that, dumpling?"

"Dumpling?"

"Yeah, all round and soft in the right places." His gaze went from my eyes down to my boobs, telling me exactly what he was referring to.

I cleared my throat so I would sound more convincing this time. "Okay."

He cocked his head in another silent question but I didn't look away. I did want him to lead me somewhere private so he could take all my clothes off. I wanted him to fuck me and it wasn't only the wine talking.

I had four hours to kill and I couldn't think of a

better way to spend them than with the man who made me weak at the knees and hot under the collar.

He stood without saying another word, taking my hand and leading me out of the bar. My stomach was a mess of butterflies, not from nerves but sweet anticipation.

I was really going to do it.

I was going to let a complete stranger have his way with me.

CHAPTER TWO

JENNIFER

Security cameras were all over the airport, making it difficult to actually find a private place. There was only one place that for sure didn't have any and he knew it too.

We entered the large disabled restroom and locked the door. It must have been freshly clean because the scent of lemons and roses lingered in the air.

Not that I had a chance to really notice.

He pressed me up against the wall, his lips on mine. I found out exactly just how soft his lips were. They pressed against my own, lapping at my mouth like he was claiming ownership.

His hands explored my body, squeezing my boobs through the fabric of my dress. He still managed to find my nipples, pinching them into tight buds that yearned for more.

Our lips parted while we gasped for breath. He recovered quickly, his mouth moving down my chin to my neck. A plethora of a kisses were stamped on my ticklish skin. I was torn between giggling and moaning with pleasure. My body was alive, brought to life by the magician holding my nipple between his fingertips.

"What's your name?" I managed to gasp out in pieces.

"Does it matter?" he asked, the vibrations from his voice being felt against my skin. He managed to get in another dozen kisses before I could speak again.

"I need to know what name to scream out when I come."

He laughed, treating me to the soft melody again. "You can call me Shaun."

Shaun.

It seemed to fit him. He was a big man, all muscles and power. Shaun was definitely a name that matched him.

"I'm Jenny," I replied, just in case he was curious. I got the feeling he wasn't, but I needed to say it anyway.

"I'm still going to call you dumpling, dumpling." He squeezed my boob again and I completely forgot about everyone's name.

He could call me whatever the hell he wanted.

Just as long as he didn't stop what he was doing.

I pulled at the hem of his shirt until he relented and stepped back so I could pull it off him. I was right about his chest. As the fabric went up it revealed the chiseled muscles of a professional athlete. Whatever he did in life, it had to be physical.

Just looking at him made me drool. I'd never been with someone so fit before and he was ruining me for all other men that would come after this one-time thing.

A thrill shot down my spine just realizing what I was about to do. Having sex with a stranger in an airport while waiting for a flight was the furthest thing possible from my usual life.

Shaun's shirt ended up on the floor before he attacked me anew. He found the zipper on my dress, wasting no time in undoing it until the fabric hung limply around me.

He slowed down just for a moment to enjoy sliding the fabric over my shoulders and watching it billow down to the floor. Thankfully I had worn my *nice* underwear, black lace as opposed to my boring old white cottons.

My boobs bulged over the cups of my bra as he drank in the sight of me. He clearly liked what he was seeing, the bulge in his jeans was impossible to miss.

His hands went to my tits, pushing the cups down so he could pop them out. It took exactly two seconds for his mouth to be where his fingertips had been. He sucked my nipple into his mouth, his tongue swirling around and making the sensations sing through me.

It was like there was a direct line from my nipples down to my pussy. It sprang to life, pulsing for some action of its own. I was curious to know what his tongue could do down there if it felt this good up here.

He worked my other breast with his hand, showing me how capable and strong his fingers were. My back arched against the wall; I was desperate to get more and more of the pleasure that I craved and yearned for.

Suddenly waiting for four hours in the airport seemed like a very short amount of time. Shaun could take his sweet time with my body, even if it meant we both missed our flights.

It would be worth it.

While my nipple was still in his mouth, his hands caressed my skin. Sliding around to my back, he rubbed circles over the tattoo I knew was there in my lower back before they moved lower. His hands teased the elastic of my panties before slipping under them.

My ass was cupped in his hands as he pulled me closer against him. I was little more than dough, pliable to whatever he wanted me to do.

We were no longer in the airport restroom, we were dancing in the clouds with the bright sun lending us heat to fuel us.

I couldn't hold on for much longer, I needed Shaun's cock in me and I needed it now. Patience was giving away to a primal need for the muscled man in front of me. I reached for his jeans and pulled open the zipper.

He wasn't wearing any underwear. His giant cock took me by surprise, making me even more desperate for him to be in me. It was as hard as his abs, ready to give me what I wanted.

What I *needed*.

What I *desired*.

"Like what you see?" he asked with amusement sparkling his dark eyes. I was momentarily embarrassed about being so brazen and caught admiring his manhood. In the next instant, he wiped all those insecurities away. "You're so sexy you made me all hard, dumpling. You going help me out here?"

My hands wrapped around his cock while he still held me close. It was a rod between us and I couldn't wait to start riding it. I lightly caressed along his length, watching how it reacted from my touch. I knew it wasn't what Shaun wanted, but I didn't want him to get it so easily. I continued caressing him until

I could see the need as fire in his eyes.

Then my grip grew tighter. I started pumping him, delighted to feel how much harder he became from my attention. I was getting him ready for me, just as he had made sure I was nice and wet for him.

He gasped with a sharp intake of breath before he stilled my hands, taking them in his. I reluctantly let go of his thick length. "That's not how I'm going to come, dumpling. I'm going to shoot my load in you or we're walking out of here right now."

I wasn't going to argue. Knowing I hadn't missed my pill in years there wasn't much to lose. "Sounds good to me."

He gave me a crooked smile of approval. He let my hands go when he was satisfied that I wouldn't do something naughty and disobey him. Walking his fingers over my skin all the way to my back again, he tugged my panties down to my knees. I stepped out of them as they fell to the floor.

His hand replaced the fabric of my panties, cupping my pussy before his fingers slid between my folds. Shaun stroked my clit, ramping up my wanton need until it was off the charts. It felt like I was going to die if I didn't have that sexy man between my legs.

For now, I had to be satisfied with his fingers. The deep need pooled in my belly, keeping me on the brink until I was just about ready to scream. I wasn't sure if I was going to be able to be quiet when I did finally get my release.

"You like that, sexy girl?" Shaun asked as he watched me intently with a smirk on his face. My head lolled back, consumed by the fire flowing through my veins. If he kept going I was going to end up as a puddle on the floor.

I could feel the orgasm trying to get a grip on me. It loitered just on the edge, laughing at me as it both threatened and begged to come forward. Whoever this man was, he had serious skills in the intimate department.

Shaun pulled one of my legs up and I wrapped it around him. I could feel the coolness of the air conditioning as it met the wetness of my pussy.

One more stroke and I would have dived into the orgasm pool. Unfortunately, Shaun had other plans. He took his fingers away from my clit, making me almost beg for him to continue.

"God, you're hot," he growled. "Your body is a playground for me. I just want to touch and ride everything."

"It's all yours," I replied. "Do as you wish with it."

"Don't tempt me, dumpling."

I wasn't joking, he could have done anything and I trusted it would only be for our mutual benefit. It felt like I was someone else, the real me was left back at the gate with my cancelled flight.

A shower of kisses were planted on my neck, sending a signal to my pussy of the pleasure my body was experiencing. Shaun was whipping me into a frenzy, igniting a fire that only he could extinguish.

"Shaun," I moaned. "God, I want you in me so badly."

"It's coming, girl. I gotta make sure you're all wet for me. Wouldn't want to hurt you."

"Hurry." I bit my lip so I didn't beg him. I'm not going to lie, some pleas were on the tip of my tongue. I needed Shaun so badly and he was dragging it out until I was soaking wet for him.

If he wanted wetness, he was getting it.

He repositioned us so his cock was ready to enter

me. I squirmed, trying to get him to fill me quicker. Finally, *finally*, he pushed into my pussy.

"Ah, your cunt, dumpling. You feel so goddamn fucking good."

He felt extraordinary. His huge cock slid into me like my body was made for him. Like we were cast from the same mold and then cracked into two people. I knew it was no use being sentimental about what we were doing, but I couldn't help it. I wanted to do it again and again. But once we left our sex room, I knew we'd never see each other again.

Maybe it was better this way.

Relationships ruined everything.

Shaun started thrusting his cock between my walls, pumping back and forth. Every time he plunged in my clit was pressed, the friction between our sexy parts causing me pleasure beyond comparison.

But it wasn't enough, apparently. Shaun weaved his hand down between us until he hit the sweet spot. His fingers tickled my clit before he started drawing long, urgent circles around the nub.

Between his cock and his hand I was in heaven

and didn't want to come back down to earth anytime soon. My hips undulated to meet his as his cock pushed deeper and deeper. With my knee still raised and my leg around him, he could bury himself as far into me as he wanted.

He wasn't just fucking me, he was fucking me *deeply*. Every few seconds I was filled to the brim with him before he pulled out and started the process all over again.

I was floating with the sensations, lifted to a higher plane of happiness than I ever knew existed. The pressure on my clit, the way he toyed with my pussy, the way he worshipped my body.

It was all too much.

The voice coming from the overhead speaker was like hearing a whisper. It wasn't enough to pull me from the state of ecstasy I was on the brink of. The whole airport would have the burned down before I stopped what I was doing.

"Show me your sexy face," Shaun growled. "I want to see you."

I upturned my head so I could look him in the eyes. They burned with desire, reflecting my own expression. He worked my clit harder, making the happiness boil in my belly and ignite.

"Cum, dumpling."

With one more flick it was impossible to stay on the brink any longer. I flew into the air as the orgasm exploded within me. It covered my bones, my muscles, my skin, and everything in between.

I bit harder on my lip as to remain quiet. As much as I kept forgetting where I was, it was still important that nobody discovered us. I couldn't do my job with a public indecency charge.

Not to mention it would make me miss the plane.

Shaun's face was a picture of concentration as his cock plunged into me once more. He buried himself deep inside, filling me to my capacity. He held himself there just a moment longer until he came.

His face was beautiful as he experienced the bliss with me. There was nothing else that existed in this one moment. It was just us, sharing a wonderful moment together.

My heart was pounding against my ribcage as I fell forward onto Shaun's shoulder. His arms wrapped around me, securing me there while we rode the wave of our orgasms.

In that moment, we were one.

The only sound in the room now was that of our ragged breaths. Adrenalin was still chasing through my bloodstream but I was coming back from the high Shaun had given me.

I'd never had sex with a complete stranger before. If it was always this good, I might decide to keep it up. The unexpected delight was more than I could have dreamed of in my wildest dreams.

Another announcement came over the loud speaker. This time I was aware enough to listen to the male voice. "This is the final boarding call for flight OT391. Please make your way to Gate Seventy-Three immediately."

Shaun and I looked at one another, both of us wide eyed as we processed the announcement. One second later, we let go of each other. His cock pulled out of me, giving me a few seconds to clean up and get dressed.

It was a race to see who could put their clothes on quicker. I had more to replace but I was faster. There was only time to gather our belongings before we made a run for Gate Seventy-Three.

We didn't even kiss goodbye.

I never even got his number.

CHAPTER THREE

PRIVATE SIMON

Afghanistan had to be the hottest place on earth. Sweat was dripping down my back as I stood in the assembly area. We were debriefing from the last mission and I was itching to get inside to the air conditioning.

"Does anyone have anything to add?" Corporal Rafter asked as he eyeballed us. I prayed nobody did, otherwise this meeting was going to be drawn out forever.

There was nothing unusual about today's mission. We went in, we guarded a hospital, we saved the place from the Taliban. A good day considering the war we were waging with the enemy.

"Okay then, you're all dismissed. See you tomorrow at six hundred hours."

Everyone started to disband, heading indoors just like I was. A tap on the shoulder stopped me. "Simon, we need to talk."

So close.

Yet so far.

I spun around. "Yes, sir."

He nodded toward the shady part of the courtyard. At least that was a small mercy. His face was grim. "Major Atoll wants to speak with you. You can probably guess what it's about."

Unfortunately, I did.

We had a traitor on the base. Someone was working with the Taliban from within our ranks. Some people thought it was me. Actually, quite a number of people thought it was me.

"I can, sir," I replied.

"Report to his office immediately."

Rafter went to leave, my voice stopped him midstep. "Sir, do you think I'm the mole?"

He faced me reluctantly. "I honestly don't know who it is."

"But you have some ideas."

"I don't know what I have." He was difficult to read but even a drunken fool could see he was lying. Rafter wasn't an idiot, he knew his troop like nobody else. The fact he wasn't reassuring me spoke volumes.

"Sir, it's not me," I said. I didn't know what else I could say to convince him. No matter how hard I worked or no matter what I did to help others, he wouldn't change his mind.

I may as well have 'traitor' stamped on my forehead.

And it wasn't only Rafter that suspected me. Watson, Cooper, Hamilton, the list went on. They all thought I was working with the enemy.

Either I was a really bad spy, or being framed.

Rafter started walking again, and this time, I didn't stop him. There no point in delaying my trip to the major's office so I headed straight there. If he was going to place me on indefinite leave, then at least I'd go home to cooler temperatures. Even the heat in Miami was better than in this bloody place.

I was directed into Major Atoll's office and told to sit down. He didn't look happy. "Private Simon, thank you for coming. I'm not going to beat around the bush and make small talk. I'm hungry and I bet you are too. So let's make this quick. Do you, or have you ever, passed on information to the Taliban or a representative of the Taliban?"

At least the answer was easy. "No, sir, I have not. Nor would I even think of betraying my country like that."

A glare from Atoll was like being struck by lightning. I held it firm anyway, not blinking. He wasn't going to rattle me, I'd experienced worse.

The silence in the room was deafening, the only noise was the slight grumbling from my stomach. I was hungry beyond words and didn't have time for this shit.

I won the staring competition as Atoll sighed. "Go on then. I hope you're telling the truth, private. I will find the bastard, you have my word on that."

"Thank you, sir."

I stood and left, letting the door close behind me.

I was tired of being asked questions like that. It seemed like they were asking them of me more than anyone else.

Fuck them all.

I was working my ass off every fucking day in the goddamn heat. I didn't need this fucking bullshit. I fumed all the way to the mess hall.

After I filled a tray I joined my comrades at our usual table. The only one missing was Watson. "Anyone heard from the groom lately?"

Rafter shook his head, conjuring up a wicked smile. "Probably still in bed with his blushing bride. Bugger got extended leave, he won't be back for another three weeks."

"Lucky him," I muttered. Watson had met his new wife, Ariana, over here in the desert. Trust him to find someone in the middle of nowhere. That man would land on his feet even if he jumped off the Empire State Building. "Maybe you'll be next."

A look of panic passed between Rafter and Kincaid. They were fucking each other but apparently they weren't talking marriage yet, even though they were engaged.

"Relax, I'm kidding," I added.

Our discussion was cut short as Major Atoll clapped his hands to get everyone's attention. He stood by the door. "I have an announcement to make. This will only take a minute and then you can all get back to your rec time."

Everyone hushed as all eyes headed toward him. He was looking even wearier than when I'd been in his office. Even though he wasn't in the field every day, he seemed more exhausted than us.

He dared anyone else to speak before he continued. "As you all know, we have reason to suspect that a member of the U.S. Military is working with the Taliban. This matter must be dealt with swiftly before any more lives are lost."

I could have been paranoid, but I was certain he looked at me as he spoke. If nobody else noticed it, they were all fucking blind.

"I have called in the U.S. Army Criminal Investigation Command to investigate the matter. We needed someone impartial to get to the bottom of this issue immediately. I would like you all meet Officer Jennifer Ramirez."

A woman stepped through the door to stand beside Atoll.

My heart stopped.

I almost choked on my tongue.

It was that girl from the airport.

CHAPTER FOUR

PRIVATE SIMON

I didn't hear another word Atoll said. All I could think about was that session in the airport restroom. I could see Jenny's naked body as clearly as I could see her fully clothed.

She was even hotter than I remembered.

In her military officer uniform, and with her hair neatly pulled back into a bun, it was difficult to reconcile the two images.

The Jenny I knew was wild and free, her hair mussed up from sex and her tits heaving with arousal. Officer Ramirez was all business, wound as tightly as her hair bun.

And she was there to find the traitor.

This was going to get rough.

No doubt Atoll and Rafter had both thrown my name on the table as a suspect. How the hell was I supposed to keep my cool when it was Airport Jenny asking the questions? My cock had begged for her every day since I flew in.

Officer Ramirez took over when Atoll finally shut up. "It's a pleasure to be here and help Major Atoll with this investigation. I promise you I will—"

Her words trailed off as we locked eyes.

She stammered before composing herself again. Nobody else probably noticed the slight blush to her cheeks. "I will do my best not to inconvenience you while I work this case. Thank you in advance for your cooperation."

She smiled and I could do nothing else than look at her luscious lips. The image of her face when she was lost in her orgasm flashed into my head.

I was in trouble.

If she was the one tasked with sniffing out the traitor, I was going to find it difficult to think straight when it came my turn to being interviewed.

Everyone went back to their food when the introductions were over with. Atoll and Jenny left, my eyes followed them all the way to the door.

It was impossible to get back into the conversation after that. I nodded and laughed when I had to, grumbled when everyone else did too. I needed to speak with Jenny. The sooner the better.

As soon as my meal was over with, I took off. She was probably assigned a room to herself in the female barracks. She wouldn't be allowed to get too close to anyone by sharing a room and therefore compromising her independence.

The female barracks was a place I generally avoided, having no official business being there. It was far smaller than the male quarters as the sheer number of soldiers was swayed one way. I didn't have a problem with women soldiers, but some men sure did.

Private Kincaid was a good soldier and it was a pity she got reassigned to another troop. Rafter was furious at first but I think he finally came to terms with it.

The only private dorm was at the end of the corridor, as far away from the bathroom as possible. I knocked and waited, hoping my instincts were correct.

No answer.

It only took a few sideways glances from a few women before it was uncomfortable standing around any longer. I stalked back to my own dorm, not seeing Jenny in my travels.

It was a long and restless night of staring at the bottom of the mattress of the bunk above me. I couldn't get Jenny out of my head. Out of all the military officers in the US, why did they have to send her? Not that I wasn't happy to see her, but her reason for being there was shit.

What would she think of me after Atoll got through with her?

Maybe she didn't *want* to see me.

The problem went around and around in my head until dawn. Sticking to the routine and turning up for work at six hundred hours was the best thing I could do. If everyone thought I was a spy, I wouldn't give them another reason to be suspicious.

We started filing into the truck, the heat already making my heavy uniform stick to my skin. I had one foot on the step before Rafter called out to me. "Simon, you're off duty."

I stormed over to him. "Why?"

"You need to report to the meeting room. Ramirez is already interviewing people and you're at the top of the list."

Shit.

There was nothing I could do, arguing wouldn't have helped. "Yes, sir."

I had to watch my troop leave without me. Instead of savings lives and protecting citizens, I had to deny charges that I'd already denied a hundred times before.

Fucking shit.

Ramirez was already in the meeting room when I arrived. But she wasn't alone, Major Atoll was leaning against the wall with his arms crossed.

I saluted my superior, hoping he wouldn't be sticking around for long. I needed to speak with Jenny alone and I doubted I would have many opportunities.

Not that I knew what I was going to say to her.

She was supposed to be a quick fuck, leaving me with a story to tell the boys. Instead, the universe decided I'd be the one who was fucked.

"Take a seat, Private," Atoll said in his usual gruff voice. That man gave nothing away but I bet he was just waiting for me to give him the ammunition he needed to fire my ass.

Jenny was all business, it was as if she'd never seen me before in her life. I wish I was that good of an actor. "Private Simon, thank you for joining me today. I know your time is precious so I promise I will be as quick as possible."

Atoll joined her at the desk, both of them now staring at me from across the table. "Well, ask away," I said. The shorter the meeting, the better. Even if I could look at Jenny's face all day and picture her screaming with pleasure.

She placed her cell phone on the table between us and hit record on her voice recording app. It was time to look and act as innocent as possible, no matter how dirty my thoughts were.

"Please state your full name and rank," Jenny

started.

"Shaun Patrick Simon, Private of the U.S. Military."

"Thank you. What can you tell me about the mission to the Taliban stronghold on the twenty-eighth day of February this year?"

There was plenty I could tell her. I could describe the mangled bodies I'd seen that were caught up in the explosion. I could detail the inhumane conditions the women and children were left to die in. There were so many horrors that day that it was enough to fill the memory on her phone.

But Jenny didn't mean those details. She wanted me to tell her all about how someone – perhaps myself – tipped off the enemy so that they were ready for us. So they had enough time to rig the place with explosives and blow up the building with us in it.

There wasn't really much to say about it. "We were deployed to the building with the objective to take control and rescue the hostages our intel said were inside. Everyone followed protocols as we entered the building. However, it appeared to be empty. It was only after we cleared all floors that Corporal Rafter suspected it was a trap. He then started to evacuate the building."

Jenny nodded along the whole time. There was no way she could really know how terrible it was on that mission. "And you lost a man in that mission, correct?"

"Yes, Private Tate. He was in the building when it finally collapsed."

She wrote some notes in her little pink book but it was angled away from me so I couldn't see. I couldn't help but think she wasn't just listening to my words but analyzing everything I did.

Was my tone of voice innocent?

Was my recollection enough to make me look guilty?

Were my eyes giving away information that I was trying to hide?

My palms were sweating and I was certain that wasn't a good sign. I thought I would be able to breeze through the interview but Jenny and Atoll were making me nervous. I'd had worse interrogators before and even they didn't have this kind of effect on me.

Jenny looked up and our eyes locked together. I was instantly back at the airport, staring into those almost-black eyes and wanting to taste every part of her. Maybe that was why she was effecting me so much.

I didn't want Jenny to think I was guilty.

She couldn't think of me as a traitor.

"So, Private Simon, I have already spoken to a few soldiers around the base. Your name keeps popping up in those conversations. Why do you think your colleagues are so suspicious of you?" She may as well have stabbed me in the gut with a knife. No wonder the brass sent her in to sniff out the snitch.

What the hell was I supposed to say to that?

Picturing her naked wasn't helping.

"I can't speak for my comrades," I said in a flat monotone.

"Surely you have some thoughts on the matter?"

"Maybe you should ask them." I was starting to sound like I was hiding something and that's not what I intended on doing in this meeting. Jenny was making me forget everything I ever knew.

"But I'm asking you, private. Don't you want to explain further? Perhaps tell me why you won't even defend yourself over these allegations?"

Major Atoll smiled and sat back in his seat with a smug grin on his face. He didn't have to say a thing, Officer Ramirez was enough for both of them.

I swallowed and took a breath. "I shouldn't have to defend myself when I haven't done anything wrong. Maybe instead of wasting time with me, you should be out there and finding the real piece of scum working with the bastards."

"So you deny the allegations?"

"Of course I do."

"For the record, please, Private Simon. Have you ever had any contact with the Taliban either directly or indirectly?"

"No, I haven't."

"And it is your position today that you have no knowledge of who has aligned themselves with the Taliban."

"I have no idea who it is."

Atoll stood. "You have this under control, Ramirez. You know where to find me if you need me."

"Thank you, sir," she replied. We both waited until the door closed behind him. "For the record, Major Arthur Atoll has left the room. Private Simon, is there anything else you would like to add for the record?"

"I am not the one you are looking for," I said. "And I have no idea who it is. The idea of having a turncoat amongst us makes me just as angry as every other soldier."

"Thank you for your time, private. This meeting has ended."

I went to get up but Jenny signaled for me not to move. I froze in place while she pointedly turned off the voice recorder.

We stared at one another for a few beats before we could speak. I didn't know what to say and all the moisture had leaked out of my palms, leaving my mouth as dry as the desert.

But I had to say something. "So you work for the Criminal Investigation Command? I wouldn't have guessed that."

"And you're a soldier. Somehow, that doesn't

surprise me."

I lifted one eyebrow. "No? What gave me away?"

Her cheeks reddened to a nice shade of rose before she pushed the words out. "Your body. It's… very nice. You are in good shape."

I couldn't stop the smirk rolling across my lips. "Just good? I seem to remember you saying something like you wanted to lick my *good* body."

Her blush deepened. "I'm sure I didn't say that."

"But you thought it, right?"

"Maybe." Her smile was as sexy as sin. I couldn't believe what was happening. There was no way that Jenny, the girl from the airport, was here in fucking Afghanistan. There was no way she was here having to listen to my brothers in arms pointing their fingers at me.

I pinched myself but I was still in that seat.

The smile disappeared in her next breath. "Are you planning on telling anyone about our… encounter?"

"No. It's nobody's business," I replied quickly. Maybe if I had never seen her again, but in these circumstances, I was going to keep my mouth shut.

She started nodding to herself, an action she seemed to do when deciding on something. There was still lots I could learn about Jenny Ramirez. And I was a keen student.

She leaned in closer and turned down the volume of her voice. "I'm required to report any conflicts of interests."

"I'm not planning on telling anyone."

"If they find out, I will lose my job."

"So we'll make sure they don't find out," I said, as if it was just as easily done as being spoken. The truth was, I didn't want Jenny to be going home so soon. There was no way Atoll would let her continue the investigation when they were trying to catch me out as the traitor. Not if they knew she was already well acquainted with me and my *good* body.

Maybe I was being selfish, but having Jenny at the base was going to make the deployment go by a lot faster. She would make conditions here that much more tolerable.

She was also more likely to leave me alone and continue her investigation into others.

Win-win.

"We shouldn't speak to each other," she started, all business again. She was even sexy as a CID officer. "We can't be seen together outside official meetings."

"Meet me at your dorm tonight," I said, throwing out the line and hoping her catch her interest.

"That's not staying away from each other."

"I'll make sure nobody sees me." That was going to be tricky, but for her, I'd do it. I would walk through cut glass to see her in private again. "Trust me, Jenny."

Using her first name seemed to shock her back to our original encounter. Maybe she was picturing me naked now, remembering how I felt inside her.

She sighed and I knew I had her on the hook. "Ten o'clock. Don't bother knocking, come straight in so you're not hanging around the corridor. You better make sure you're invisible."

"You have my word."

My day suddenly got a lot better.

CHAPTER FIVE

OFFICER JENNIFER RAMIREZ

I was a complete idiot. There was no way to rationalize what I'd done. From the moment I arrived in Afghanistan, there was only one name that had continually come up in conversations about the traitor.

Private Shaun Patrick Simon.

Aka Tank.

Aka the man I had sex with in an airport restroom.

What was I thinking?

I had never broken protocol before. There were

reasons why I had to report conflicts of interest. How was I supposed to be unbiased when I kept picturing the biggest suspect pinning me up against the wall?

First a one-night stand, and now breaking protocols. Shaun was having an effect on me that I couldn't explain. He was a magnet that kept scrambling my brain and pulling me toward him.

But I wasn't going to sleep with him again. We were *not* going to have sex ever again. I needed to stay independent.

I was going to get myself in trouble and lose my career. Even worse, I was going to bring shame to my very strict, very Christian family. This I knew with certainty, yet I had still agreed to meet with Shaun in my dorm.

I was not going to sleep with him.

The floor was going to be worn out from my pacing while I waited for him. I both dreaded and couldn't wait for him to arrive. Ever since that moment in the airport lounge, I couldn't get him out of my head. I'd spent the entire flight over thinking about him and all his rippling muscles.

Seeing him again was like a gift, until I realized he was the one everyone suspected was guilty. I'd never been more torn apart. I just hoped I would be able to pull myself together soon.

The door suddenly opened as Shaun slipped into my dorm. He quickly closed it again, standing in front of the only exit and giving me a dangerous sexy smirk. Every part of my being wanted to kiss those damn lips.

I was not going to sleep with him.

The mantra kept spinning around and around in my head. It turned so many times that I could almost block it out as white noise.

Shaun rushed at me and I completely forgot what I was supposed to remember. I was swept up in his arms, surrendering my mouth to his. My body responded instantly, pulsing deep down in my pussy until I was soaked.

He was wearing a khaki T-shirt, so tight it contoured to every one of the muscles I knew it hid. His pants were camouflage, tucked into his heavy black boots. Around his neck, dog tags swung loosely.

My hand went up to tangle in his hair. It was the standard cut all male soldiers wore but he made it all his own. I loved feeling the softness run between my fingers.

My own hair was tied back in a bun, the requirement for female officers. Shaun pulled at the ties until it came apart and my long hair cascaded down my back.

He flicked all the buttons of my blouse until they were free, pushing the cloth over my shoulders until it fell away. He cupped my boobs in his hands, feeling the weight and enjoying the hard nipples that gave away my intentions.

"I never thought I'd see you again," he mumbled. It almost sounded like he was talking to himself rather than me.

"Neither did I," I said.

"When I saw you in the mess hall yesterday, I thought I was dreaming."

I laughed. "And you were about the last person I expected to see."

He kissed the hollows of my neck. "I am so glad you're here."

Any further words were silenced as his mouth pressed onto mine. I moaned happily, feeling sated from a hunger I never realized was there. Shaun made me feel so alive, I wanted to bask in the feeling forever.

His hands worked the zipper on my skirt before he removed it from my body completely. Shaun tugged his own shirt over his head and quickly undid his pants. We were both left in our underwear.

"Turn around," he ordered.

A sharp thrill ran down my spine at the command. I had no idea what he was about to do but I couldn't wait to find out.

I faced the bed, a few moments later I could feel the heat of his body behind me. My bra fell away only a second later. His hands instantly kneaded my tits, relaxing me enough to lean back against him and enjoy the sensations.

His mouth traced kisses all down the back of my neck and to my shoulders. Goosebumps completely covered my skin, betraying how much effect he had on me. I was practically jelly in his hands.

"I could never get enough of you," he said,

speaking so close to my ear his breath tickled. "You are who all my filthy daydreams are about."

I wanted to switch my brain off but I couldn't ignore all the alarm bells completely. "We shouldn't be doing this. Someone might catch us."

"We're not going to get caught, Jenny." His hand slid down my stomach and didn't stop as it slipped between my folds. He tickled my clit, giving me beautiful waves of pleasure. "Do you really want me to stop?"

I hesitated. He wasn't playing fair. With his hand between my legs it was impossible to send him away again. Not when I wanted so much more than just his fingers.

"Just enjoy the ride then," he whispered. "Your sexy body was made for this. And I was made for giving it to you."

I believed him. He knew how to touch me better than I did. Every one of his motions was enough to make me as horny as hell. The entire military base and all of its responsibilities faded away when he was close by.

His hard cock pressed into my lower back. He was

just as excited as I was, ready to come together and milk one another for the ecstasy our bodies were capable of. I couldn't imagine sending him away now.

His fingers toyed with my clit, rubbing long lengths up and down with enough pressure that I couldn't move. His other hand continued to knead my supple breast, rolling the nipple between his fingers with expert precision. I was in heaven and Shaun was my drug.

"I want you to come, dumpling," he whispered. Just hearing his nickname for me again was like a shot from heaven. I completely leaned back on him and felt all the tingles he was making pulse through me.

"Are you ready to come for me?"

I was. I was so ready.

He tugged at my nub and there was no more waiting allowed. The orgasm completely shattered me, making my knees go weak as I felt the strong arms holding me up and against his muscled body.

His hand cupped my pussy underneath my underwear, waiting for me to rise out the ecstasy while I was lost in my own world. Every part of my being was alive and aware of all the places our skin was touching.

Shaun's lips were suddenly on my neck again, tickling and adding to my excitement. Blood pumped through my heart at an extreme rate while the waves crashed and ebbed from my belly upwards. There was nowhere more fun than being under Shaun's control and command.

"Did you like that, dumpling?"

I nodded, my breath hitching in my throat. "Yes. More."

Shaun chuckled. "You'll get more, don't you worry about that."

His hand slid out of my panties before he pulled them down my legs. He let me go just long enough to remove his own boxers. I turned around so I could take him all in. His muscles were as hard as his cock, inviting me to taste every part of him.

"Uh-uh," he tsked. "Turn around. I'm going to put you over that bed and fuck you from behind. You have a problem with that?"

I shook my head side to side, chewing on my lip

to stop the wide grin from spreading around my face. Having sex with Shaun was more fun than should be legal. I faced the bed again before his hands touched my back and pushed me forward gently.

When I was leaning on the bed, he spanked my bare ass. The surprise hit me harder than he did, making me jump. He rubbed the area with his open palm, sending a new wave of thrilling delight ripple through me.

"You're a naughty girl, aren't you?" he asked, spanking me again.

"Yes," I breathlessly replied. I never imagined being spanked would be so erotic before. I wanted to be bad, just so he would continue to do it.

I was used to being the disciplinarian in my job. I told soldiers what they could and couldn't do, being under someone else's control was the complete opposite. I was giving all the power to Shaun and I reveled in it. He could do to me whatever he wanted.

Every time he spanked me, his hand drew lower. He was no longer tapping my ass but between my legs. The change in sensations was exquisite. From the sharp stings on my cheeks to the beautiful taps on my pussy. He was driving me insane, taking me to the next level of arousal I'd never known before.

"Spread your legs wide for me, baby. I'm going to fuck your little cunt, you can put that in your report."

Shaun pulled my legs further apart until I was splayed for him. The anticipation grew to extreme levels. I knew what kind of pleasure he could give me and I was ready to beg for it if necessary.

His fingers massaged my clit. The spanking was over now, it was time for the deep touching that led to complete satisfaction. I needed it, I didn't realize how much until this moment.

My needy cunt had been aching for Shaun ever since our first encounter. It was a need deep within my belly that nothing else could satisfy.

His hand was replaced with his cock as he positioned himself. He ran his hard down the length of my pussy, coating himself in my juices so he would be able to slide right into me.

Our bodies stilled as he readied himself at my entrance. Shaun took his time sliding into me. Inch by magnificent inch, he eased between my walls and filled me with his thick manhood.

He felt massive, reminding me of the only other time we had fucked. His large cock had surprised me then and it did the same again now.

I felt myself stretch to take him in as my hands gripped onto the bedsheet, holding on like I wanted to hold onto him.

Shaun sucked in a breath as he started thrusting. His hands were on my hips, holding me in place so he could piston his cock in and out of me. I felt every movement stoke my fire, far faster than it should have.

This magnificent soldier was so certain as he moved our bodies together. There was no hesitation, he knew what he wanted and he was ready to take it from me. And I was more than ready to give it.

"Fuck, you're tight, dumpling."

I was already breathless, too taken away to reply to him. If I opened my mouth now I feared I would start yelling in pleasure. We weren't supposed to be doing this, nobody could ever know what was happening in this room.

Not now and not ever.

It was too late to turn back now, not like I really

wanted to. In the heat of the moment I was prepared to give up everything so I could surrender to this man. No matter what the cost.

One of his hands circled my hip as he reached down to toy with my clit. His fingers were insistent, rough, and determined. My pussy pulsed for him, yearning for the release that was standing on the precipice.

"God, you feel good. I'm so close. We're going to come together, you hear me? When I say cum, you are going to cum."

"Yes," I breathed.

His fingers rubbed on my nub, circling the sensitive area like he owned it. He pressed onto my clit with a grunt. "Cum, dumpling. Cum now."

There was no way to resist. His cock thrust into me before he swore under his breath, losing himself while his load of cum let lose deep within me.

I only barely registered what he was doing as I felt myself be swept away with the orgasm. The fire that had been blazing in my belly let loose on the rest of me, making me a human inferno. Every part of me was alive and screaming out the sheer joy singing through me.

My elbows couldn't keep me up any more. Shaun let go of my hips as I fell onto the bed. The waves continued to wash over me while the orgasm ran its course. There wasn't a part of me that wasn't relaxed and as soft as putty.

Shaun pulled out of me and I felt his absence deeply. It only lasted a second before he laid on the mattress next to me, pulling me to his side and wrapping his arms around my shoulders.

"I still can't believe you're here," Shaun confessed.

"I can't believe *you're* here. I never thought I'd see you again after the airport."

"Are you sorry you did?"

I definitely knew the answer, I didn't have to think about it. "No. I've been thinking of you ever since. I was angry that I didn't get your phone number."

Shaun chuckled. "The crazy thing is that I was too. I couldn't believe I walked away from you with nothing but the memory. It was a good memory, but I wanted to see you again. And again."

"Just to have sex?" I probed.

"No, baby. I wanted more of all of you. I found

myself daydreaming about you. I imagined a whole conversation between us."

"What was the conversation about?" I was very keen to hear exactly what Shaun had on his mind. I needed to hear it all, even if I was afraid of what he'd say.

"I wanted to say I thought, for the first time, that I believed in love at first sight." Shaun's words hung in the air like bunting, decorating the stark dorm. He *loved* me? Surely I couldn't interpret that any other way than what he had clearly stated?

"You fell in love with me when you first saw me?" I had to clarify, I couldn't breathe again if I didn't.

"In the airport lounge. You looked at me and it was just like I knew." He paused. "And that sounds like the lamest story in the world. Forget I said anything. The military psychologist says I have attachment issues because of my father. You can't believe anything I say."

I nudged him in the ribs gently. "I believe whatever you say."

"How can you be sure I'm telling the truth?" he challenged.

"Because I felt love at first sight too."

Silence settled around us as the heaviness of those words lingered in the air. Maybe they weren't direct declarations of love, but they were good enough. I just hoped I wasn't making the biggest mistake of my life.

We said nothing further as we laid together, waiting for our hearts to return to their normal beats after the workout. Having sex with Shaun was a beautiful thing, but loving him was tiring too.

While my head rested on his chest, and his heart echoed in my ear, I hoped I wasn't wrong about him. I'd never risked losing my job before and conflicting emotions were starting to take ahold of me.

I feared asking him the one question I really needed an answer to. Because I might not like what he said afterwards.

Maybe he *was* guilty of being a traitor.

Maybe I was sleeping with the enemy.

CHAPTER SIX

PRIVATE SIMON

I fell asleep in Jenny's bed.

It was the stupidest thing I could have done. As soon as we'd fucked, I should have left and pretended it never happened. We were both skirting a line that couldn't ever be crossed.

If she wasn't so goddamn sexy I might have been able to resist her. But the woman was a walking goddess and I wanted to worship her at any opportunity I got.

I woke up in the early hours of the morning. So early that I might have been able to make it back to my bunk before anyone even noticed my absence.

Jenny was fast asleep, her naked body cuddled up against mine. It took everything I had to be able to walk away from her now. If I had my way we would never leave this bed again.

I wriggled out, repositioning her so she wouldn't be disturbed. Surely she would understand why I had to leave without saying goodbye. Discretion was the watchword now, nobody could find out what we'd done.

"Are you leaving?" Jenny mumbled as she opened her eyes. The messy just-got-fucked look suited her. With tussled hair and a husky voice, she could have easily convinced me to stay and play a while longer.

"Yeah, it's going to be morning soon," I whispered in reply.

"Is it you, Shaun?"

I crouched down next to the bed, brushing her hair from her forehead. "I'm here, it's me."

"No." She shook her head. I suspected she was still mostly asleep. "Is it you that is the traitor?"

I'd felt a kick to the guts before and it was nothing compared to her question. "Go back to sleep, dumpling. We'll talk again soon."

She closed her eyes and I left her there, hoping she didn't remember the conversation in the morning. She was asking dangerous questions and it wasn't something we should talk about while the glow of sex was still shimmering on our skin.

Walking back to my bunk was nerve-wracking. I expected to be caught around every corner, but thankfully nobody was up yet at that God-forsaken hour.

By morning I was still tired, even though I'd managed a couple of hours worth of sleep. I lined up with the rest of my comrades and had breakfast. There was no trace of Jenny in the mess hall.

We lined up at our station right at six hundred hours. Rafter ticked us off the list as we boarded the truck. I kept waiting to be called off duty again like the day before but nobody appeared.

I tried to keep the smug I-just-got-laid grin off my face. Even though everyone in that truck thought I was the traitor, they were still my brothers in arms. It was hard not to spill the beans and tell them everything.

Our mission today was to clear a section of the city known to be infiltrated by Taliban members. They were taking houses off their owners and using them as hideouts. The locals were being kicked out and terrorized by their own people.

The truck rumbled through the dirt streets. Luckily we weren't relying on stealth for this mission, the enemy would be able to hear us coming a mile off.

We were all dressed in full battle armor for this mission. The bullet-proof vest weighed a ton, as did my utility belt. My helmet was making my head bead with sweat and my boots were ready to run, even if not built for comfort.

When I first enlisted in the US Military, I was an excited eighteen-year-old. I was ready to take on the world and show the buggers who had control over this battlefield. Even though that was only five years ago, it already felt like a lifetime had passed.

My beliefs weren't so clear cut now. I was jaded, not with the military but with everything. The world wasn't as black and white as I expected it be. Sometimes choices made now would have been horrifying back then.

We had two trucks for this mission, needing to split up and take the neighborhood at opposite ends. We were hoping the Taliban wouldn't be able to escape, that we could round them up and take them in.

Which was naive.

The Taliban never let themselves be captured. They always put a bullet through their brains before they allowed that to happen. They preferred death over being used a weapon.

I understood how they felt.

The second truck passed us and continued on to their location. They signaled through our communicators that they were in position shortly afterwards.

"Okay men, let's get the bastards," Rafter said before jumping out of the truck.

We followed him, guns at the ready. Adrenalin surged through my blood, making all my senses sharp and ready for action. The heat was oppressive, surrounding us the moment we were out in the sun. Even sunscreen didn't stop us getting burnt, the motherfucking sun was a special kind of evil here.

It took only nine minutes of us stalking through the streets before the first bullet was fired. The Taliban were shooting at us from inside a home. It looked like all the others in the street, like a happy family might be inside and living their ordinary lives. If the fuckers didn't take it, maybe they would have been doing that.

We spread out and took cover behind another house. Rafter's hands were flying about wildly, silently communicating his plan with us. We were to surround the house at all four points, then storm in if we couldn't take them out beforehand.

There was no way to tell how many of them were inside. By the time intel trickled down to our ranks it was pretty thin. No numbers, just that there were a bunch of them doing bad shit and they needed to be stopped.

I might not have agreed with a lot of what this war was about, but I did hate anyone who caused civilians to be caught up in it. Kids didn't need to see the reality of war, neither did the innocent. This was between us and the Taliban, nobody else.

I took off with Rafter as we ran side by side. He had assigned me to him as soon as his girlfriend was transferred to another platoon. He said it was because I was the youngest member of the troop and he wanted to teach me as much as he could.

That was bullshit.

Rafter was certain I was the traitor and he was keeping an eye on me so he could find proof of my guilt. He'd done the same thing with Kincaid, kept her real close until she proved she was capable of handling her own.

I was sick and tired of constantly being watched. Half the time I wished they would just send me home so I could get a break from the drama. I was a good soldier, I'd never given them any reason to suspect me of being a spy.

I hadn't even reported the unsanctioned fuck sessions Rafter had had with Kincaid while she was in our troop. I caught them practically naked and never said a word to anybody about it. I could have, but I didn't.

Fat lot of good that loyalty got me.

"Get down!" Rafter cried out suddenly. I ducked

down without question – just in time to see the dirt behind me kicked up with a bullet.

"Thanks," I muttered.

"How many do you think are inside? My best count is five."

I studied the house. There were at least two guns positioned at the window. They were still firing in a few directions so there had to be more. "Five sounds about right, at least that many anyway."

His radio crackled and the others reported in that they were in position. It was go time. Rafter counted down from three on his fingers and then we all started firing.

My gun was a lethal weapon in my hands, its presence made me feel invincible. There was only one other thing that made me feel that way – sex. I enjoyed being in control with a gun and my cock.

A shower of bullets were sent to the windows of the house. We were all firing, hoping to land a few shots on the enemy. At that point escape for them would have been impossible. We all knew they were going to die one way or another.

Either that, or we would be the dead ones.

Hopefully we had the numbers we needed to make it out of here alive.

More bullets came back at us, forcing us to retreat to the next house back so we could use the concrete walls as a shield. It also gave us a better angle where we could see the back window and everything that happened behind it.

The target house's drapes were all closed, making visibility an issue. Our ammunition tore them to shreds in a matter of seconds, exposing the fuckers hiding behind. Their numbers seemed to dwindle as we kept firing.

Eventually, everything was silence.

Eerily so.

This couldn't have been their single hideout in the neighborhood. We couldn't get cocky and think it was all over. Their comrades would be around, watching us until they made their move.

"We're going in," Rafter said, both to me and his radio. We walked in a crouching position, trying to keep our heads as low as possible in case someone decided to take them off.

All teams moved for the house in unison,

storming through the doors all at the same time. It was dark inside, even with the redecorating we did with the drapes. Nobody flicked a switch, both because there probably wasn't electricity and because we didn't want the enemy seeing anything.

Our flashlights got us through. In the living room were a pile of bodies, fresh gunshot wounds reddening their tunics. I checked every one of them, making sure none were only pretending.

"Clear." The word echoed from every team as we combed through the house. There were no survivors to capture and torture information from. The Taliban shrank in numbers.

The mission may have been successful so far but it was definitely not over. If our intel was correct there were many more houses just like this one that we would need to clear.

War seemed so pointless. Every day we were sent on missions just like this one and we had been doing it for years. Sometimes we won, sometimes we lost, the whole thing was starting to jade me. It seemed like there was no end in sight and even if we could all return home, did that mean we won, really?

I didn't think so.

Rafter's radio crackled to life with the strained voice of a soldier. "Backup needed urgently on Tibrez Street." He repeated the request a few times, each one more panicked than the next.

The corporal didn't need to tell us what we had to do but we waited for the formal order anyway. "Everybody over to Tibrez Street. Let's move, soldiers."

Our illustrious leader showed us the way. We could make it faster on foot so we ran east in the hope of getting there in time to help with whatever was going on. It took a lot to rattle these guys so whatever it was, they really needed us.

The house they were in was obvious as we got closer. There were military trucks haphazardly parked all around it, each one devoid of its soldiers.

"Everybody spread out. We go in through all doors," Rafter yelled out.

I stuck close to him as his teammate for the day. Wherever Rafter went, so did I. We stormed into the building through the front door, heading into God only knew what. My heartbeat stopped when I saw what was inside.

Jenny.

With an arm around her neck and a knife pressing against her jugular.

How the hell she was in that position was beyond me. She should have been back at the base, well away from this kind of danger. I wanted to scream so I could find the one responsible for the situation. A civilian, even an officer, should have been in a safe office, not in the arms of the fucking Taliban.

Everyone was still and silent in the living room. The guy holding her was slowly edging backwards toward a set of stairs. They probably led upwards to the second floor. Anything could have been up there, including an infestation of Taliban members.

At least a dozen high-powered guns were facing him but he knew nobody would shoot. Not when he was using Jenny as a human shield. I knew differently, they *would* shoot if they got the right opportunity.

All they needed was a clear shot.

I'd been in this situation before, but hostage negotiations weren't my responsibility. Only certain soldiers received that kind of training and I wasn't on the shortlist yet.

I was putting all my hope on Rafter and wishing he would hurry up and say something so we could get Jenny out of the situation.

I'd never been so scared before.

Seeing somebody I cared deeply for with a knife to her throat was quite possibly the worst sight I'd ever seen. A million thoughts ran through my mind, all trying to work out how to kill the fucker before he could kill Jenny.

Every second that passed by was one too many.

"Let her go," Rafter said carefully. "You're outnumbered here, you're not going to move one more inch before someone takes you out. Do you want to take your chance with the snipers or are you going to release the woman and end this without you being dead in the end?"

I couldn't even be sure if the guy spoke English. We needed an interpreter but there wasn't going to be time to wait for one to arrive from base. Jenny would be dead by then, along with every daydream I'd had about her and our future.

The man started speaking in Dari with an accent too thick to even pick up the basics of his words. Everything he said sounded like a threat, regardless of us speaking different languages.

I knew when someone was bloodthirsty.

He had that look in his eyes.

Jenny's eyes were wide open with fear, the emotion rolling off her in waves. We all would have felt the same in her position, no matter how brave we all pretended to be.

"She's not who you want," Rafter continued. If he actually thought he could get her out of this situation with words, he was a bigger fool than I thought he was.

I levelled my gun at the man, trying to see if I could get a clean shot without injuring Jenny in any way. He kept moving around, constantly keeping himself on his feet to thwart any snipers like me.

"Let her go and you can have me," Rafter said. "She's a civilian, this isn't her fight."

Again, he was answered with a garbled smattering of words we didn't understand. Most likely he was telling us exactly what he thought of us.

It was all taking too long and prolonging Jenny's misery. Something needed to be done and clearly Rafter wasn't going to do it.

I needed to do something.

And I needed to do it now.

CHAPTER SEVEN

OFFICER JENNIFER RAMIREZ

His breath smelled like tobacco.

Not the kind people smoked back home, but something stronger. Like he'd taken to eating the stuff, coating his tongue with it until he reeked.

He also reeked of sweat.

And not in the good way.

I should have been focused on something else but my mind knew if it did I would go crazy. Maybe even *do* something insane to try and get out of the situation. So I was concentrating on the smells and trusting in the soldiers huddled around in the small room to save my life.

"Let her go," Corporal Rafter said. Not that it seemed to be doing any good. If anything, it only made the arm around my neck grow tighter.

Images from my past didn't flash in front of my eyes like I was promised they would. Maybe I wasn't as close to death as I thought. Yet I could still feel the cold steel of the knife as it pressed onto my throat.

"Drop your knife and let her go or we will shoot you. You are not going to get out of this situation alive without her being safe first."

Major Atoll said it would be good for me to get out in the field and observe the men. Like perhaps I would be able to stop the traitor by his actions rather than his words. I knew it was a risk leaving base but I never imagined I would end up as a hostage either.

"Don't make me shoot you now."

The moment I had seen Shaun storm in with the others, I had felt relieved. He was there, and every time he was around, only good things happened. I knew he cared for me enough to rescue me.

At least, I thought he did.

Fear pulsed through my veins while I tried to remain still. If Rafter was planning on shooting his way out of the situation, they would need me to be still. Otherwise we were both going to end up dead.

My captor started yelling in Dari. I hadn't heard it spoken by someone with the native tongue before. My language teacher had made it sound much smoother and slower. This man was throwing words out with no regard for their fluency.

He didn't care if he was being understood.

I managed to pick up a few words here and there, again using distraction as a technique to quell my rising panic. He was telling them they were all 'infidels' and were going to 'burn in hell' for their crimes against Allah. He said nothing could save their souls now. I was also fairly certain he'd thrown in a whole string of swear words but I couldn't be sure – we didn't officially learn those in class.

All of a sudden the man pulled me tighter, almost cutting off the oxygen to my airway. I had to stand on tiptoes just to keep my head still attached to my body. If he continued on, he wasn't going to have a live hostage to negotiate with.

My hands automatically went to his arm, trying to claw it from my neck. Black spots were starting to blur the edges of my vision – I was running out of air.

"Let her go!" Corporal Rafter screamed.

The man went backwards up the first step of the staircase. He dragged me along with him, momentarily using his knife hand to steady himself against the wall. Stars were starting to burst in my vision, making everything blurry.

Everyone started yelling at him as the knife returned to my throat and started digging into the soft flesh. It stung like a bee and remained throbbing around the knife. The tickle of blood oozing from the wound started to go cold on my neck.

He tugged me up another step.

Everyone yelled some more.

I could hear voices from up above, men on the second level of the house. No matter how hard I tried to listen, I couldn't be sure how many of them there were. It sounded like many.

Enough to outnumber our soldiers?

Maybe.

Through the whole melee, one set of eyes stood out above all others. Shaun was looked at me down the barrel of his gun. In that fraction of a second, realization dawned on me.

He was going to shoot.

I had only a moment to process the information before everyone was silenced by the crack of a gun. It wasn't loud, but everyone knew what had happened.

The arm around my neck slackened.

The knife fell away.

I was pushed downwards, tripping down the steps without being able to find any purchase. I landed on the floor in an undignified heap while chaos was making its home around me.

All the soldiers were moving, trying to get up the stairs while those upstairs tried to get down. I crawled to the wall and huddled there, making a small ball with my body and hoping it was enough to stay out of the fray.

"Are you alright?" It took a moment for me to understand that the voice was speaking to me. "Jenny, are you okay?"

Shaun's brown eyes were a glow of comfort in all the madness around me. I nodded and he remained a moment longer to see if I was lying.

He took off again when more shots were fired upstairs.

My shoulder was covered in blood. When I felt the red stickiness, I panicked. But there was no pain in my body, my captor had been shot but Shaun had missed me. He was a hell of a sniper.

Still, I wondered whether he had disobeyed protocol by acting when there was still dialogue being exchanged between the parties. It was crazy to be thinking so logically in such a traumatic time but it was all I could do to not focus on the terror that had seeped into my body.

I hated that I was having such doubts about Shaun. My heart said one thing and my brain was saying another. If so many people thought he was secretly working with the Taliban, there had to be some reason behind it. My college professor used to always say there was truth behind every rumor.

Shaun had just saved my life.

I needed to give him the benefit of the doubt. At

least for now.

The sound of boots stomping and the smell of gunfire assaulted my senses. It continued on until soldiers finally started making their way downstairs again. I was grateful to see every face, hoping none of them had lost their lives in the house.

Shaun helped me stand as relief washed over me. "Did everyone make it?" I asked, holding my breath until I heard the answer.

He nodded, his face red from the stifling heat. "Yeah, everyone got out. There were eighteen of them up there but not one decided to live today."

Eighteen dead people were a high number of lost souls, even if they were the enemy. Our superiors told us it was them or us, even knowing that didn't make it any less difficult.

Shaun helped me out of house and to the truck. Nearly everyone was still inside, cleaning up before we could move on. "What are you doing out here?" he asked gruffly.

"The major thought it would be good for me to observe in the field. He said I would stay out of harm's way."

He punched the truck. "I'm going to kill him. You could have died in there, Jenny. Nowhere here is safe. The moment you leave the base you are fair game. The Taliban don't care who they kill as long as their blood is red."

I'd never seen him so angry before. "Hey, it's okay, I'm okay. You saved my life, everything is fine."

"No, it's not. I almost…"

"Almost what?" I prompted.

He dragged his gaze back to me, the fire within him slowly simmering down to pain. "I almost lost you. If I did, I just don't know what I'd do."

His confession surprised me. He may have worshipped me when we were naked but I wasn't naïve enough to think he held strong feelings for me fully dressed.

I didn't know what to say.

Thankfully, our conversation was interrupted as Corporal Rafter called Shaun back to duty. He gave me one last look. "Just promise me you won't leave the base again."

"I won't." Nothing would get me through that

gates again, not after this deadly sojourn into the Afghanistan desert.

I was returned back to base where I remained in my dorm room for the rest of the day. I told everyone I was fine, but when I was alone, the tears I'd been holding onto flowed in earnest.

Part of me expected Shaun to knock on my door in the middle of the night, but he didn't. I wasn't sure what that meant, if anything.

The next day, I returned to the meeting room given to me for my investigation. Corporal Rafter was scheduled to meet with me so I threw myself back into work. That way I didn't have time to ponder what could have been my fate yesterday.

We sat down and stared at each other for a moment. Sometimes it was amazing what you could learn in the silences. Corporal Rafter was young for his ranking, but he was fully capable according to Atoll. He sat with a straight back, his hands on his thighs. He was showing no casualness to me, it was all business.

Clearly, he wasn't going to be the one to talk first. I started the voice recorder and kicked it off. "Please state your name and rank.

"Matthew Edward Rafter, Corporal of the U.S. Military."

"Are you aware of the reason for my presence here on base?"

"Yes, ma'am. Suspicions have been raised about a possible leak in the ranks."

"Do you agree with those suspicions?" I asked. I always enjoyed getting straight down to the nitty gritty of the situation and not wasting time. Everybody here had a job to do and I didn't want to keep good soldiers from their troop.

"Yes, I do."

"Why?"

He hesitated a moment, those three letters potentially about to open up a big can of worms. When he finally spoke, it felt like his suspicions weighed on him. "There have been several missions lately that have resulted in the Taliban acting in a way that would suggest they knew we were coming. They had things prepared in such a way that couldn't have been just a coincidence."

It was pretty much what Major Atoll had told me.

"You don't believe in coincidences?"

"I don't when it repeatedly happens. Once or twice could be coincidental, but not when it continues."

He was right, but I needed to hear the words from him. I couldn't lead him in any way, otherwise the interview wouldn't stand up in the trial that would follow an arrest.

"Give me some examples," I said.

He ticked the items off on his fingers. "We stormed the medical clinic and it was rigged with explosives. Then there was the incident at the hospital. Plus the school, they knew we were coming. Nearly everywhere we've gone, the Taliban have been ready."

"They could just be paranoid and prepare for any attack."

"They could," Corporal Rafter said, pausing. "But I don't believe they can be that prepared. Their resources aren't enough to be ready for everything."

I wrote down some notes about his demeanor that wouldn't be picked up on the voice recorder. He seemed quietly confident in everything he said. His body language was open and honest.

I liked him.

He seemed like a straight-up kind of soldier and I appreciated that. My presence at a base wasn't usually welcome as I investigated our own. Anyone that assisted my case was welcome in my books.

"Do you have any opinion about who the traitor could be?" I asked. It was the sixty-four-million-dollar question that I needed to find an answer to.

Corporal Rafter leaned forward, letting out a deep breath as he showed his reluctance at naming names. "I think it might be Private Simon, but I can't be sure. Honestly, the idea of any one of us working against us, makes my gut twist."

Even though I'd been expecting him to name Shaun, it still stabbed at my heart. "What makes you think he is involved?"

He shrugged and his gaze met mine. "I don't have any proof."

"I'm not talking about proof. What has he done that has raised your suspicions?"

"We're all soldiers here, we signed up to protect our country and lay down our lives if necessary. That kind of dedication means we have a certain attitude toward our country. Simon seems to have lost that belief in what we're doing."

That was new. The way everyone else talked about suspects, they described incidents and tales of tattling. Nobody else discussed the attitude of soldiers.

"You think he's jaded," I prompted, careful not to lead him. I had to stay impartial, especially considering I was sleeping with the soldier we were talking about.

"I think he's lost the drive that we need to carry out our duties to the highest standard."

"Have you had to discipline him?"

He shook his head. "No. He does his job, he just doesn't take any pride in it. It's like he's going through the motions but doesn't feel it in his heart. Does that make any sense?"

"Yes, it does." I'd seen it plenty of times in my relatively short career before. Once you lost the drive, you lost the motivation.

I tried to think back to yesterday, in that house with the Taliban. I had seen Shaun in action with his troop, did it seem like his heart wasn't in it? He had held the gun with confidence, taken the shot when nobody else did. He saved my life, but was he just 'going through the motions'?

My heart wanted to scream *no* but I wasn't so sure. Was he just doing his job? Or was he doing it because it was me that was in the line of fire?

Everything I did with Shaun, and everything I thought about, was dangerous territory. I didn't know how I was going to be able to do my job when people kept pointing their fingers at the man I was fucking.

I should remove myself from the investigation. I should walk straight to Major Atoll's office and report my conflict of interest. If I didn't, and it was Shaun that was guilty, I wasn't convinced I would be able to convict him.

I was screwed.

That was all I knew for sure.

It was difficult to keep everything going on inside from showing on the outside. "So, in your opinion, you think it warrants a further investigation on Private Simon?"

"Yes, I do, ma'am."

"Is there anything further you would like to add?"

"No, ma'am." He paused and then added, "Except that I'm sorry you have to be here at all. I'm Simon's superior, it was my responsibility to keep him on track. If he is the traitor, then I should be charged with showing a lack of due care."

"Thank you, Corporal."

I switched off the voice recorder when he left and my shoulders sagged. More than anything, I wished someone would walk into my makeshift office and point the finger at someone else.

It couldn't be Shaun.

He was a good man. I'd seen it in his eyes, in his tender strokes when he brushed the hair from my face and tucked it behind my ear. Surely he couldn't be working with a force that killed innocent people?

The door suddenly opened and I pushed back all the emotions that were welling up. Major Atoll stepped into the room and closed the door again.

"Officer Ramirez," he started. "You found the dirty bastard yet?"

"I'm still conducting interviews, sir."

His lips pursed together until he looked like he was sucking on a lemon. "I need this rat found so I can have him charged. Every day that passes is poison out here. I need my men to be united, they can't be looking at each other and wondering if it's them."

"I'm well aware of the time pressures, sir."

"We need someone arrested."

Talk about pressure. "I'm working as fast as I can, sir. I promise you'll be the first to hear when I have a case against someone."

"Work faster, officer. We have lives at stake here." He didn't say another word before he left.

I had one good suspect.

I could have told that to Major Atoll.

But my heart wouldn't let me.

I really was screwed. I needed to talk with Shaun, at least gives him the heads up. He deserved that, at least.

CHAPTER EIGHT

PRIVATE SIMON

My usual scan of the mess hall revealed Jenny in the line. It was a relief to see she was okay, hopefully that meant she'd been on the base all day and not out there getting hurt like yesterday.

I figured I could probably spot her in any crowd, even one of millions. She had this way of attracting my gaze, like she was a magnet and I was pure steel. I liked it, even though I had no right to. After all, we weren't officially together.

Grabbing a tray, I pushed into the line to be beside her. Nobody called me out on it, nobody dared. Apparently it was known that I was working for the enemy, so people tended to give me space now.

"How was your day, officer?" I said, catching Jenny's attention.

She startled slightly, her eyes only flicking to me briefly before they returned to the food. "It was quite long, but I'm sure it wasn't nearly as unpleasant as yours was."

"I don't know, being inside all day seems pretty unpleasant to me." I smiled but she didn't return it. Something was wrong and it instantly made my insides turn.

"At least I was safe," she said. Jenny could have been talking to anyone, definitely not the man she'd shared a bed with recently. I could feel her cold shoulder even in the desert.

We shuffled down the line while we grabbed food along the way. All the things I wanted to talk to her about suddenly vanished from my mind. I wasn't prepared for her icy reception.

Did she think I was the traitor?

What fucking lies had people been telling her all

day?

"Is it you?" she asked quietly, in such a small voice that I wasn't certain she meant to say it out loud. No matter how many times the question was asked, the sting never got easier to handle.

"No," I replied, the only word I knew how to form.

"Are you sure?"

"Meet me later," I said. We inched along the line a little more before she finally shook her head.

"I can't."

"What?"

"I just can't."

What kind of a game was she playing? The last time I saw her she was fine. *We* were fine.

And now she didn't even want to meet with me?

"I think we need to talk," I insisted, it came out unintentionally as a low growl.

"I said I can't," she replied.

We reached the end of the counter. Jenny picked up her tray and sat at a table by herself. I couldn't go and sit with her, it wouldn't take much for the wrong person to see us together and put the pieces together.

I sat with Rafter, Cooper, Salinger, and Ridley. The conversation at the table ended the moment I sat down, leaving an awkward silence.

"You can continue talking about me if you want," I said. It was supposed to be a joke but it didn't sound much like one. I was pissed, not only at Jenny but at everyone.

I was ready to lay down my life for all my brothers in arms and now they couldn't even *talk* to me? What kind of treatment was this? They'd never seen me do anything wrong but had decided I was guilty anyway.

It was Jenny's job to find the traitor.

Maybe she wasn't looking very far.

My shitty day was only getting worse. I was looking forward to lights out just so I didn't have to keep being treated like shit by everyone I knew. Tomorrow would probably be the same but at least I would be able to get some reprieve from it.

"We weren't talking about you," Rafter said. He scooped some carrots into his mouth and kept talking. "In fact, we were talking about the Superbowl. My money's on the Broncos winning this year."

He was probably lying. If I was in a better mood I might have been able to keep up the ruse and play along. Not tonight, not after the fucking awful day I'd had.

I shoveled food into mouth, eating fast enough that I would probably have indigestion later on. As I cleared my plate, I stood. "The Broncos have no chance."

Silence followed me all the way out of the mess hall.

Apparently staring at me was a thing now. The craze seemed to be rampant in the ranks with everyone doing it as I moved.

Excluding Jenny, who was doing everything she could *not* to look my way. Apparently that magnetic attraction only went one way.

They could all go to hell.

It was still too early to go to bed and I was riled up enough to get myself in trouble. The rec room was the only part of the base that didn't seem like it was full of people. Private Kincaid was the only one in there. She wasn't glued to Rafter's side, which was a change.

I flopped onto the couch and tried to get lost in the television. Kincaid had some bad reality show on which definitely wasn't my idea of fun. Still, I could stare at the screen with nobody hassling me.

Or, at least, so I thought.

"What's gotten you all brooding tonight?" Kincaid asked. She didn't look at me, keeping her eyes fixed on the television.

"Haven't you heard? I'm the fucking traitor."

"Shouldn't you be up to all kinds of shenanigans then? You don't have a clandestine meeting with a man dressed all in black tonight?" She smiled and gave me a sideways glance to make sure I knew she was joking.

"Nah. That was last night." I couldn't help but smile back. Out of all the hostility and whispers I'd put up with all day, Kincaid was a nice change.

I'd always respected Kincaid. She'd proven herself several times over when we shared a troop. It didn't matter that she was a woman, she could definitely hold her own both out in the field and at base.

She was also Rafter's fiancé, which I couldn't forget. Anything that I said to her could very well make its way back to him.

"You sure it's safe to be talking to me?" I started. "My guilt could rub off on you. Wouldn't want to tarnish that good image of yours."

"I'm pretty sure I did that when you caught me making out with Rafter," she replied, still with that lilting grin on her lips.

She was very easy on the eyes, Private Kincaid.

Very easy, indeed.

"I never told Atoll about that, you know. I never told anyone, just like I said I wouldn't."

"I know."

"Really?" It sounded like she was lying, just to make me feel better. I'd been denying everything for weeks now and it seemed nobody was listening. I was surprised to still be invited to Watson's wedding, I thought he might have taken it back after this whole shitty mess came up.

"Really," Kincaid said. "Just like I know you're not the one that internal affairs officer is looking for."

"How can you be so sure? Unless it's *you* she's searching around for."

She punched me on the shoulder. Kincaid had a decent right hook. "I know because it's not something you're capable of. You're a good soldier, Simon. You don't deserve to be tarnished like you are."

"Well, thank you, Kincaid. You are officially the only sane one in this entire goddamn place." I meant it too. "Seriously, the only thing that bugs me more about the whole thing is that everybody is too busy pointing their fingers at me that the real bastard is getting away with it."

She nodded in agreement. "Who do you think it is? Present company excluded, of course."

"I have no idea. I wish I did, then maybe I could convince them to look at someone else."

"Have you been interviewed yet? That woman is scary."

I chuckled, because the idea of Jenny being scary was laughable. Sexy, sultry, gorgeous, intelligent, were all words I would rather use to describe her. Scary was down the list by about a hundred rungs.

"I was interviewed the other day," I confessed.

"It seems like she's trying really hard to get to the

bottom of the matter." Kincaid seemed genuine, like she wasn't just saying things to make me feel better. It was nice to have a sensible conversation with someone. "She might have a whole range of people she's looking into."

"I doubt it. Everyone wants to pin it all on me. It would be an easy case if enough people all say the same thing. I'm probably going to lose my career, maybe even go to jail."

"They need evidence to charge you, Simon." Kincaid made it seem like it should have been obvious. "They can't go on word alone. Considering you didn't do it, they won't be able to find any proof. They won't be able to prosecute."

I wanted to believe her. God, did I want to believe her. But all I kept thinking of was what about if they *did* find proof?

It was possible.

Crazier things have happened.

No matter how much someone thought they were doing a good job, it was only human to make an error. Given enough time to really look into things, anything could be discovered about a soldier.

Including me.

There were plenty of things I didn't want Jenny knowing about me. Unfortunately, she had carte blanch to open up the pages of my life and study everything with a magnifying glass.

I stood to leave, no longer wanting to talk to anyone. "Let's hope they find the bastard so they stop pointing their fingers at me," I said.

Kincaid gave me a mock-salute as I left. She returned to watching her reality show while I stalked back to my dorm.

After washing away half the Afghanistan desert from my body, I hit the sack. I didn't really feel tired but my mind was weary. I needed a rest, otherwise I wasn't going to be able to get up in the morning and do everything I needed to.

I heard all the guys come in and lay down eventually. It was shortly after the dorm was full that I finally drifted off to sleep.

My alarm went off at four a.m. It felt like I'd been asleep for only the same duration as a blink of an eye. There were no such things as days off out here. They worked our asses off and then a bit more.

Nobody else was up yet, which was exactly the point of my early morning rise. I crept around the sleeping quarters and gathered my things, choosing to dress in the bathroom so I didn't wake anyone.

I needed to see someone.

Any they weren't going to wait for me.

CHAPTER NINE

OFFICER JENNIFER RAMIREZ

Sleeping in my bed didn't feel the same without Shaun but I couldn't invite him back in. We were playing with fire that would surely burn at least one of us.

After all, I felt like an inferno when around him.

Proof enough.

I'd tossed and turned all night, uneasy about the way I had treated Shaun in the mess hall. There were too many people around to explain why I couldn't meet with him. I didn't want to give him the brushoff but maybe that was for the best anyway.

My hand was on the door to the meeting room when I was stopped by Corporal Rafter. His face was red and he seemed flustered. "Officer Ramirez, have you seen Private Simon this morning?"

"Why would I know where he was?" My face flushed with heat. Surely he didn't know what was happening between us? Could he have seen Shaun slipping away from my dorm the other night? Did he notice the stolen glances between us? The panic alarm went off in my head.

He gave me a bemused look before he continued. "I'm asking everyone. Nobody has seen him anywhere and he wasn't in his bunk this morning. Have you seen him?"

Embarrassment about my reaction made my face flush even more. "No, I haven't seen him. Maybe check the mess hall, he might just be running late."

"If you see him, please tell him to report to his station asap."

"Will do, Corporal."

He nodded and then hurried down the corridor, stopping everyone he encountered along the way. I hurried into the room and sat down, taking some deep breaths so my face would return to its normal color. I was going to give us both away by acting so crazy.

My ass had only just reached the seat when Major Atoll stormed into the room. He had a way of demanding attention without saying a word. He could make anyone quiver in their boots with just one glance.

"Major, good morning. What can I do for you?" I asked politely.

"You caught the bastard yet?"

Here we go again. "No, sir, there have been no further updates since we spoke yesterday. I have more interviews today. I'm certain I will get to the bottom of it in due course."

He snorted. "That's not good enough, officer. I need a result now or this whole base is going to go to hell. Get out in the field today, I'm assigning you to Rafter's troop so you can observe Simon firsthand."

"Sir, after the last time—"

"That's an order, Officer. Get down to the vehicle bays immediately."

Major Atoll stomped out of the room before I

could protest further. You would think almost getting killed the first time would have relieved me of field observations. Apparently my life as an officer of the military wasn't worth all that much to him.

The idea of going out on a day's missions with Shaun and his troop made me feel sick but also excited me. My job wasn't exactly riveting and a part of me always regretted not enlisting for the more physical roles. While I still served my country, sometimes it felt like I was just on a constant rotation of paperwork.

I hurried down to the vehicle bays, searching for Corporal Rafter so I could report in. I had to wait with his troop for twenty minutes before he finally joined us. His face was an even darker shade of red than mine was earlier.

"Simon still hasn't showed up?" He addressed the question to the whole troop. Everyone replied with the negative. "Fucking hell. I've been all over this base and I can't find his ass. We're going without him. Officer, what are you doing here?"

"Major Atoll ordered me to join you today."

"Just what I need. Fine, let's move out."

I didn't dare say another word. Between Atoll and Rafter, I couldn't see my day getting any better. Maybe there was something in the food that made them all cranky.

The last thing I wanted to point out was the fact that if Shaun wasn't on the mission, my own mission of observing him wasn't going to happen. I was better off just keeping my mouth shut. And who knows? Maybe I would find another suspect to add to the list.

Private Cooper assisted me with putting on some protective gear. The bulletproof vest and helmet were extremely heavy and only added to the heat of the desert. We all filed into the truck and then left the safety of the base gates.

Corporal Rafter explained to the group as we drove that we were patrolling the marketplace today. They had intel that warned of some members of the Taliban using the markets to trade illegal weapons. If the wrong people spoke to the right traders, they could obtain dangerous guns that would be used against their own people and us.

The soldiers spoke a language all of their own

while on the mission. They communicated with hand gestures and moved as stealthily as panthers. I had to give my all just to keep up with them.

The marketplace was an open-air area about the size of a few blocks – it was hard to tell exactly. Ordinary people did their shopping while we, in full camouflage uniform, walked alongside them. They paid us no attention, so used to seeing the military presence that we were a simply part of the scenery now.

It all seemed so surreal. If the army patrolled markets back home like this, someone would put it on YouTube. Even I wasn't so easy with all the guns the guys held, and I was on their side.

If I was a tourist, the marketplace would have been idyllic to walk around. All the vibrant colors of the fruit and spice stalls begged for my attention. The fabrics of the tunics that hung in racks were alluring. It was difficult to imagine such sinister trading was also being done behind the curtains.

We were right in the thick of things when all hell broke loose. A gunshot rang out, so close to us I thought one of us had to have been taken out by the bullet.

Everyone in the troop reacted immediately, crouching down and pointing in the direction of the noise. I followed suit, my heart pounding against my ribcage as true fear pumped through my blood.

Another crack of a gun.

Followed by another.

And then a constant rumbling of the sound, so loud it could be mistaken for thunder.

The soldiers around me formed a protective barrier, keeping me behind them, but I was still in the line of fire. I'd never been so scared of anything in my life before – and that included the other day, at least it was only a knife used there.

People screamed and scattered as they were caught up in the fray. I saw several of them cry out as they fell to the floor. Blood started to flow on the concrete and mud floor of the marketplace.

The bullets seemed to be coming from all directions. The troop fired back, but only when they spotted a target. Our side didn't agree with just blindly shooting, not when there were so many civilians still in the middle of it all.

"Stay down," Rafter warned beside me. I hadn't been planning on doing anything else. I liked my head where it was, I didn't fancy it being blown apart anytime soon.

"We're surrounded," Cooper said to the group. The voices all travelled around me like I was in a dream rather than really living the nightmare.

"Bastards knew we were coming."

"Look for a gap. There has to be a gap."

"Hamilton's down!"

"Fuckers are just shooting and hoping they hit someone. It doesn't matter who."

"Ridley, get back!"

"Base, this is Rafter. We are in urgent need of backup at mission location. Repeat, urgent backup is needed."

"They're not going to get here in time."

"We'll keep fighting until we're dead then."

"Fuck, Hamilton has been shot!"

"He's gone, there's nothing we can do to save him now."

"Fucking hell, there's blood anywhere."

"Samson, do a recon."

"All points are covered, sir. There has to be at least two dozen of them."

"Bloody hell."

"Hold on for backup, men. We are not going to die out here today. It's not going to happen."

Everything went quiet then. Not the bullets, but the voices. The troop were focused on not dying, their concentration was required. I huddled in the middle of them, trying not to think of what would happen if they all went down.

Because then I would, too.

I didn't dare raise my head to look around the area again. From my hiding place I could see some of the bodies sprawled on the ground. Vacant eyes stared at the sky like they were waiting for salvation.

My stomach was tied in a knot and time seemed to stand still. I felt useless in amongst it all, I wanted to help but there was nothing I could do. And to think, I had been excited about the mission. It was so stupid of me to forget about the danger that the soldiers live with every moment of every day.

There was no way I could observe the men to search for the traitor. Each of them were doing their jobs just to stay alive. There was only a united front here, nothing more and nothing less.

Corporal Rafter's radio crackled to life. "Backup on location. Request brief."

Rafter replied with a hurried explanation of where they were and what was going on. The relief on the soldiers' faces was palpable. They'd done it, they'd survived until backup arrived.

My relief was palpable too.

After a few more minutes, each one feeling like hours, the men were able to stand. The gunfire fell back as we moved as a unit through the market. The backup soldiers had come in behind the Taliban members and taken out enough of them so we could move.

We were still outnumbered, but no longer trapped. I was ordered back to the truck while the soldiers attacked to reduce the enemy's numbers.

My whole body was shaking while I listened to the barrage outside. It was impossible to tell which side was winning, if any. At the end of the day all both sides were doing was adding to the body count.

There were no winners in war.

Shaun had said that to me the other night and now I fully understood what he meant by it. It was fine to sit at home and see the updates on the news, but it was a whole new ballgame when you were actually on the frontline. My heart went out to all the soldiers.

They were gone for hours before finally leaving the marketplace. Privates Hamilton and Ridley had both lost their lives in the carnage. We had to take their bodies back to base in the truck. I kept my gaze forward so I didn't have to look at their lifeless corpses.

It was selfish of me to be grateful that Shaun wasn't on the mission today. I shouldn't have valued his life over any of the others, but I did. I couldn't help it. My heart beat for him and no amount of denying it would change that fact. It was something I needed to keep deeply hidden inside.

I'd never been so happy to see a military base before. Only when we passed through the gates did I breathe a sigh of release.

We climbed out of the vehicle, dirty, bloodied, and traumatized. I leaned against the fence for a moment to take it all in.

"You okay, officer?" Corporal Rafter asked. His face was brown from dirt and his vest was covered in someone else's blood.

"Yeah, just a little…"

"Take it easy tonight and forget everything you saw."

I wished it was that easy. My feet started moving but I walked like a zombie. I wasn't sure what I was supposed to do now. How did you return to normal after seeing what we'd seen out there?

When people you'd only spoken to that morning, had died?

I ended up in my meeting room office, needing some time alone so I didn't break down in front of everyone. My head went down onto the desk and I let out the tears I'd been holding in.

More than anything, I wanted to be in Shaun's arms. He would whisper sweet lies into my ear and make it all better. I needed that kind of comfort, that sense of safety you could only find in a lover's arms.

The daylight outside turned dark and still I sat there. My stomach was rumbling, telling me it was past dinner time.

I wiped my face before I returned to the public realm. The mess hall was beckoning me with the smell of mass-produced food. I didn't care what it tasted like, I just needed it in my stomach.

The hall was relatively empty as I made my way through the line quickly. I sat at a table by myself and tried not to think of the two soldiers who wouldn't be joining us tonight.

I said a prayer for them and hoped some higher force heard me.

The moment my tray was returned and I was ready for a long-overdue shower, I ran directly into Major Atoll. "There you are. I need to talk to you in my office, now."

I trailed after him without argument. He was understandably wound up. Corporal Rafter was already in his office and waiting for us.

The major closed the door behind us. "Private Simon is missing," he started. "After what happened today out there, that is proof enough of his guilt."

"I don't understand," I said. My brain was too foggy for the discussion.

Rafter explained further, "We were ambushed in the marketplace today. The Taliban knew exactly when we would be there and knew exactly how to kill us. Simon hasn't been seen all day. If he was on that mission, he would have been ambushed too. He knew to stay away and now he's hiding with the enemy."

The evidence *was* there, it did seem very suspicious. I could understand why they wanted an arrest quickly after losing our own, but I still had to follow my protocols.

Or was it just because it was Shaun that was making me hesitant?

"Issue an arrest warrant immediately, Officer Ramirez," Major Atoll said. There was no room for argument.

I nodded. Maybe by the time we found him, the emotions wouldn't be riding so high.

Shaun's absence was troubling for more reasons than one. If he wasn't the traitor, he might be in serious trouble. At least issuing the warrant would motivate people to help search for him.

I hoped he was okay.

He had to be.

CHAPTER TEN

PRIVATE SIMON

Everything was quiet. It was like I had stepped into an alternate universe where nobody talked. I didn't really know *where* I was, let alone who was with me.

I was supposed to be meeting Kincaid to do additional training with her but she was nowhere in sight when I arrived in the gym. Maybe I should have been wary when the note she left for me was typed and not hand-written.

Kincaid would have asked me face-to-face.

Hindsight was a bitch.

There had only been one voice I'd heard since this morning and they hadn't been back for a while. I wasn't sure how long exactly, but it felt like at least a day.

Everything was black.

Fucking black.

My head was entombed in a black hood. The fucker had placed it over my head about two seconds before he hit me in the back of my head.

I'd fallen to the ground like a sack of potatoes, completely knocked out on impact. I was in a sitting position now, but I had pulled myself up to that pose after the man had left. The moment I heard the click of that lock, I'd tried to get up.

Sitting was the best position I could move to.

My hands were tied together in front of me. I'd always joked about trying out some ropes in the bedroom but never outside of it. And certainly never with a male son-of-a-bitch.

I wished I'd caught a glimpse of him. Just one little hint about who had done this to me and I would track him down and show him what happened when you gave a soldier reason to seek revenge.

In my current state, with my hands tied together and my ankles bound, I wasn't in any position to get back at him anyway. I'd get my revenge but I would have to get myself out of the situation first.

I tried to picture where I might have been but there were no clues given to me. I'd been unconscious when moved from the corridors of D Block and I couldn't see, smell, or hear anything now. I could have been anywhere in the world for all I knew.

The click of the lock grabbed all my attention. I thought I might have imagined it.

Until I heard it again.

Something bumped against the door and then it squealed open. My whole body froze as I waited for what would happen next. It could be someone rescuing me, but I wasn't that naïve. Chances were better that this person was here to hurt me.

I could feel their eyes on me and the single set of footsteps told me it was probably just one person. My best guess was it was the bastard that had knocked me out.

Feet shuffled.

Someone breathed.

Metal clinked on the floor.

"Who's there?" I said to the darkness. "Tell me who you are so I know who to kill when I get out of here."

"I don't think you're the one in a position to make threats right now." It was a male voice, the same one I had heard in the split second between being hooded and punched.

"I'm a member of the U.S. Military and I order you to state your name and purpose."

He laughed under his breath. "What a coincidence, I'm a member of the U.S. Military too. Do you really think that's going to get you anywhere here, soldier?"

I was trapped between having a sense of self-preservation and wanting to shoot my mouth off. I had to bite my tongue before I said something that might get me killed.

"What do you want then?" I asked, fishing for more information. I racked my brain trying to place his voice with a face but I just couldn't make the connection. Perhaps it was my concussion that was making my mind a little fuzzy.

"I want everyone to pay for being infidels," he said with a growl in his voice. His words sent a cold shiver down my spine. I probably shared a table at mealtime with this man, all the while he was devising a plan to kill us all.

There was nobody I could look at in the base and imagine them capable of something like this. While I knew there had to be somebody, I guess I always held hope that the past events were all just coincidences.

Proof of my stupidity was standing right in front of me. He was the man that should have been investigated for traitorous actions, not me. Jenny should be hunting down *this* man.

Jenny.

I hoped she was okay and this bastard hadn't done anything to her. One way to escape detection was to take out the officer undertaking the investigation.

"So what am I?" I started. "A hostage? A future murder victim? Tell me what your grand plans are for me. I'm assuming you have some of those, of course. I'm sure you didn't take me for my sparkling personality and tight ass."

He leaned in closer, I could feel the heat from his body roiling off him. He dropped his voice to a cold whisper. "You're my scapegoat."

The penny dropped as ideas and memories clicked into place. It wasn't just a coincidence that everyone thought I was the traitor.

They had been led to believe it was me.

This fucker had framed me.

Anger boiled through me, ready to make me burst and forget all about my sense of self-preservation. My hands balled into fists but they couldn't get anywhere near him while tied together.

"I hope you go to hell," I said through gritted teeth. If he was closer, I would have bit him. I would have done any damage to him I could, if I could move.

He started laughing and there wasn't one breath of warmth in it. My blood ran cold, and for the first time since I was taken, I thought these might be the last moments of my life.

The guy stood up, his boots shifting and then stomping as he reached the door. "There's a knife on the floor. I'm done with you."

Another squeak of the door and he was gone again. I didn't waste a minute to start scrambling for the knife. I found it, but clutching it between my fingers and using it was another thing entirely.

My grasp on the handle was brief as it kept sliding through my fingers. Every time I dropped it, I went looking for it again. Over and over again I followed the same routine.

Find the knife.

Try to cut the rope around my wrists.

Drop the knife.

I wasn't going to give him another chance to kill me. My life depended on me freeing myself so I could get out of wherever he was holding me.

The thought of the whole bid for freedom being a game to him sprung to mind. He could be on the other side of the door with the rest of his terrorist friends, just waiting for me to walk to my death.

But I couldn't think about that. I had to believe I was going to get out of there alive or I wasn't going to be able to do anything at all.

The image of Jenny pushed aside all the horrible

thoughts. Even if I could just spend one more night with her, it would make my difficulties seem worth it. She was going to be directly in the traitor's spotlight and I couldn't let him hurt her.

Hopefully I wasn't too late.

I had to get to Jenny and warn her about the man. She had to know how dangerous he was and help me search for him. I would be able to recognize his voice if I heard it again, I'd locked it into my memory so I could use it later.

I *would* get him.

He would not be able to hurt Jenny or any other of my comrades. We were together in this war and he was against us.

Traitors deserved to die.

Plus, that fucker had framed me. Out of the hundreds of soldiers on the base, why had I stood out above them? Why did they hone in on me and decide that I was the one that would take the fall for him?

I didn't want to think of that right now. The reason why I had been targeted specifically might not be an answer I wanted to hear.

The rope loosened around my wrists. Finally, I had cut through. The moment my hands were free, I pulled the bloody hood from my head.

There were shelves around me, each piled high with supplies – uniforms, towels, bedding, toiletries. They were all neatly lined up in the orderly way of the military.

I was still on base.

In a fucking supply closet.

My attention went to the rope biding my ankles as I cut them free. Now that I was able to use both my hands, and see what I was doing, it only took seconds.

Everything tingled in my limbs as I used the shelves to help me stand up. I'd been in that one position for God only knew how long and my blood was now returning all feeling.

Half of me expected the door to be locked, but it wasn't. My kidnapper had just merged back into the crowd of soldiers and nobody was any the wiser of his illegal acts.

It felt like I should be emerging into a different world after being in the supply closet for so long. But nothing else had changed for my comrades. They'd all gone on their missions today, worked hard in the heat, and were now itching to get some food in their bellies.

No matter how I tried to blend in, it felt like I was doing everything to stand out. My legs were stiff and wooden, my fingers felt dirty and were bloodied from working with the knife. Nothing about any of it felt real or normal.

Rafter was the first face I recognized in the sea of men. He was heading straight for me and I sagged with relief. I would report everything that happened to me. I would outline everything the traitor had said to me and then they would all realize that I wasn't the one they were looking for.

They would have to believe me then.

I would take them to the supply room and show them the ropes I had left on the floor. They would see the knife I used to cut myself free. And I would tell them about the voice I had heard.

Finally, I would be able to clear my name.

"Private Simon," Rafter started as soon as he reached me. I couldn't wait to have my story told so he could start to search for the man.

"Yes, sir. I have to explain—"

"You are under arrest for treason against the U.S. Military and gross acts of terrorism. You have the right to remain silent, anything…"

I stopped listening as I shook my head and tried to get my thoughts in order. Surely he wasn't saying what I thought he was saying?

I was under arrest?

They got the wrong person. As soon as I explained to them what happened, they would realize their mistake and we'd all laugh about it one day. 'Remember the time when you thought I was a terrorist?' Then we'd have another beer and thank God we caught the real bastard.

"You've made a mistake. It wasn't me, I can explain everything," I said when Rafter had got to the end of his spiel. "You just have to listen to what I have to say."

"If you want my advice, private, keep your mouth shut." Rafter grabbed me on the arm and started steering me toward the few cells we kept on the base. I didn't want to go with him but I also didn't want to have the discussion in the middle of the corridor, either. The actual terrorist could easily have been listening.

It felt like a very long walk to the prisoner cells. We must have passed every single soldier on base as they gawked at us. Everyone thought I was guilty anyway so they couldn't say it was an unexpected turn of events.

Of course, the one person I *did* want to see wasn't anywhere to be seen. "Is Officer Ramirez okay?" I asked just as we reached the cells.

Rafter pushed me into one and pulled shut the bars so I couldn't escape. "She's in with the major. I'm sure she'll be paying you a visit soon. Remember my advice about keeping your mouth shut. You'll be doing yourself a favor."

He slammed the door to the cells on his way out and it echoed ominously around me. I was the only one being held prisoner. The fact that it was in my own base was just depressing.

How had my comrades, the men I fought alongside every day, really think I was capable of sentencing them all to death?

I guessed it was redundant to think they just didn't like me in the first place. Perhaps that was why the real traitor had chosen me as the mark. Pick someone that didn't have any friends, someone who would have nobody to stand up for him.

I wanted to scream with frustration. I knew Rafter had told me to keep my mouth shut but that was the last thing I wanted to do. I want to yell my story from the fucking rooftops.

There was nothing but a bucket and a bench in the small cell. I sat on the bench and hoped I would be out of there before I needed to use the bucket. The worst cells back home were better than the best cells over here.

Time slowed for the second time that day. Hours could have been minutes and days could have been hours. I sat there, trying to find the most succinct way to tell them of their mistake. They wouldn't listen to me if I started ranting and raving. I would have to remain calm so I could get it all out and capture their attention until the very end.

When the door finally did open, it was a relief.

Officer Jenny Ramirez stood there.

She had a mixture of disappointment and anger on her beautiful face. It was difficult imagining her in the throes of ecstasy now. She looked like a formidable foe when in work mode.

"Jenny, you have to—"

She cut me off with a single raising of her hand. "You are entitled to a lawyer being present. I think you should wait until we can organize that for you."

"No, I'm not going to be silent. I didn't do anything, you have to believe me. If you'll only listen to what I have to say, you'll let me walk free from this cell."

"I can't," she said apologetically. I hated that this was mentally hurting her. "It's my job to build a case against you. When you went missing today, and then everything happened at the marketplace, I didn't want to believe it. But it's my job and I have to do it."

And just then…

My heart broke into a million little shards.

CHAPTER ELEVEN

OFFICER JENNIFER RAMIREZ

"I don't care about a lawyer," Shaun said. His was piercing me with his unblinking and unwavering eyes. Maybe if he kept it up, I could discreetly tell his lawyer to go for insanity.

"You should."

"Will you just listen to me, please? I don't care if you have to record it, I don't care what charges there are. All I care about is telling you everything. I need to do that, I'm not guilty. Please, Jenny."

It was that last please that got to me.

Shaun was the man I was falling for. He was the

stranger in the airport who had given me the most passionate moments of my life. He deserved a few minutes, at least.

"I have to record this," I warned, pulling out my cell phone. He nodded and I hit the *record* button. "This is an interview conducted in the base prison cell between Officer Jennifer Ramirez and Private Shaun Simon."

I settled the cell phone on the bars between us and nodded for Shaun to begin. He took a deep breath and told me a story I could hardly believe.

It was my job to get to the truth and remain impartial. The greatest trait we were supposed to have was our independence, followed by an unwavering need for justice. Everything in the logical part of my brain told me that Shaun's story was little more than a series of outrageous lies to cover for the immoral truths he wanted to keep a secret.

That was how I would have concluded my case if I didn't know Shaun better than I should have. I had been intimate with the man, I had seen him at his most vulnerable. The beating heart in my chest wouldn't allow me to believe he could be responsible for the deaths of so many comrades and civilians alike.

When he stopped talking, I had to force my emotions down to ask the questions I had to. "Is that everything?"

"Yeah, that's it," Shaun said. He seemed tired and weary after getting out all the details. It was a look in his eyes that he couldn't fake. At least I knew one thing for sure.

"It's a very convenient story," I started, praying that he would understand that I had to do my job. "It explains your whereabouts today and why everyone is pointing their fingers at you. What evidence do you have to support it?"

His eyes flashed with anger for a moment before he gained control of himself again. "Go to the supply closet, you'll see the rope, hood, and knife there. I left it all after I cut myself free."

"I will do that. What other evidence do you have?"

"Nothing. I have nothing," he admitted. I wished there was something he could use to clear his name. Any little piece of evidence to prove his story. I couldn't very well report to my superiors with just a feeling in my heart.

"Think really hard," I urged him, far stronger than I would have to any other prisoner. "Is there nothing else that backs up your story?"

"It's not a story. It's the truth, Jenny. I swear it's all true. Someone is framing me and he's on the base walking around and beating his chest with the victory. Please believe me."

I picked up my cell phone and concluded the interview. There were so many things I wanted to say to Shaun but the security cameras would pick them up and then I would be taken off the case. If Shaun really was innocent, then he didn't have a hope if I got sent home and another officer came in to finish what I started.

"Sorry," I mouthed to him before I turned away. I could feel the burning of his eyes on my back the whole way out.

I headed straight for the supply closet he had indicated. Even though I'd only been on base for a few days, it was pretty easy to find my way around.

The closet door was closed and it creaked when I

opened it. I stepped inside as my gaze roamed over all the shelves and then the floor.

There was nothing there.

All the supplies were neatly stacked in the way only the military could accomplish. There was plenty of toilet paper but no knife, hood, or rope. Everything looked exactly as it should have.

I had really wanted to find those items. I would have gladly gone back to Major Atoll and said we had the wrong man in custody. But without that evidence, what did I have?

What *choice* did I have?

If I explained why I thought he was innocent, we would both lose our jobs and face disciplinary actions. It wouldn't prove his innocence, it would just guarantee a new officer would cover the case. I couldn't do that. I had to protect our secret.

By the time I reached Major Atoll's office, I still hadn't determined what I was going to say. His assistant waved me through and then I stood in front of the man responsible for the safety of all his men.

"Good job this evening, Officer Ramirez," he started. "Now we can get back to winning this war without the enemy always expecting us."

It was make or break time. "Sir, I don't believe Private Simon is the person we are looking for."

"Everyone says it's him."

"He could be being framed, to take suspicion away from the real traitor."

Major Atoll waved it away. "Officer, if it looks like a duck, walks like a duck, and quacks like a duck, it's a duck. We have our man."

"But, I think—"

"He's guilty, Officer. Case closed. I will organize transport to take you both home to the U.S. where he will face the consequences of his crimes."

I needed a new tactic, my current one wasn't working at all. "Sir, I need some more time to gather evidence. I'm not convinced the traitor is working alone. Think about it, could one man have been able to cover his tracks so well? I just need a few more days to be sure. Without strong evidence, he will never be convicted."

At least he didn't interrupt me that time. He pursed his lips together while he considered it. My heart pounded in my chest while I waited. Once we left base, there would be no chance to help Shaun in any way.

I continued on, trying to sway his mind a little further. "What about if we let him go? He could lead us straight to his accomplice or the Taliban. If he's guilty, he probably knows about more Taliban strongholds than you do. Wouldn't you like to take them down at the same time? Think how good that would be."

Major Atoll stared at me, his face unreadable. He might have seen through my bullshit or he might have been eating it all up. I didn't know the man well enough to interpret his expression.

Finally, he started nodding. "You have the rest of the week. If we don't get results before then, you're both on the next plane home. Simon will be placed under covert twenty-four-hour surveillance. He needs to believe he's free so he makes a mistake. I hope you're right, Ramirez. Otherwise we are making the biggest mistake of our careers."

"Yes, sir, I understand."

He flopped down onto his seat, deflated. I knew how he felt, it had been one of those days.

A few days was all I had now. Every minute counted and the clock was already ticking down. There was a lot of work to do.

But step one was to get Shaun out of his cell.

CHAPTER TWELVE

PRIVATE SIMON

Relief.

When Jenny came back and told me the charges were dropped, I felt nothing but relief. Maybe now they could catch the real traitor and throw his sorry ass in jail. Hell, they could hang him in the mess hall for all I cared.

"Thank you," I said to Jenny as she held the cell door open for me. If we were anywhere else, I would have kissed her. And that would have only been the beginning of what I wanted to do to her.

"Don't thank me," she said quietly. "Just be

careful."

She was acting weird, she had been ever since she returned. I wanted to ask her what was really going on but there were cameras everywhere in the cells. I didn't want to give anyone a reason to question her.

I swallowed down everything I wanted to say to her and left. They'd only had me locked up for a few hours but it already felt like weeks.

One glance back at Jenny and I could tell there was something wrong. She was trying to smile but it was nothing like the one I knew she was capable of. All her sparkle had dulled and I feared it was me who had done that to her.

My stomach growled, telling me I had to go by the mess hall, then do whatever else I needed to. I headed straight there and tried to ignore all the glares I was getting along the way. Obviously news of my arrest had filtered freely through the ranks until the whole base knew about it.

Nobody stood near me in the line for food. It was like I existed in a bubble and everyone else had to stay outside of it or they would be tainted with my stain. For the first time since joining the army, I felt separate from my comrades. They wouldn't take a bullet for me now, they would use me as a shield to save themselves.

It was going to take them a while to trust me again, but when they arrested the real traitor, it would go a long way toward repairing that relationship.

I took my tray to a table filled with soldiers. If I sat alone, they would talk about me. I didn't want to hide away, I wanted them all to see me free and not fazed by the whole thing.

The way I saw it, if I skulked around, they would think I had something to hide. Being out in the open and myself, that was as good as screaming my innocence at the top of my lungs.

As I sat there eating I listened to the voices flowing around me. I was trying to hear the voice of the fucker that tied me up earlier and left me in the closet all bloody day. Unfortunately, none of those I could hear were a match.

It would only be a matter of time.

If I didn't find them, then Jenny would. She was good at her job, she wouldn't let him get away with what he was doing. The little stunt he'd pulled on me was minor compared to all the innocent lives he'd cost.

"Hey, Simon," Private Jackson called out over the table. "Did they let you out for good behavior? Or did you break out of the clink?"

"They let me go because I didn't do it," I yelled back. Every other conversation died as they all listened to us. A knot was starting to form in my stomach. This kind of attention was not what I needed right now.

"Didn't do it, or they couldn't prove it?"

"Yeah, Simon. How bloody do your hands have to get before they can finally arrest you, huh?"

Jackson had started a floodgate of swipes, emboldening all the soldiers to join in the discussion. "I swear, you are the only person around that can work with the fucking Taliban and get away with it."

"Do they pay you in little virgins? Information for a girl?"

"You can't really think you can get away with this, right?"

"If they think I'm going to work with a bastard traitor, they've got another thing coming. There's no way I'm serving next to you anymore."

They were getting nastier as they all tried to outdo one another with barbs. If they were only joking, I would be able to take it. However, they were all deadly serious and I couldn't handle it.

I stood up. "You want to come here and say that, Jackson? Huh? Piper, Dekker, Goodes? Come on, come say that to my face."

Jackson stood up, his chair falling backwards and making an almighty crash on the floor. If people weren't paying attention before, they certainly were now.

He stomped toward me, the muscles of his neck tight and his hands clenching into fists. I stood my ground, refusing to back away. Shying from this fight now was as good as admitting I was weak and guilty. This was more than just standing my ground.

"I'll say it again, you're a motherfucking prick. Is that clear enough for you?" Jackson said through clenching teeth. I'd rarely seen him so angry before, and certainly not with me. Clearly they couldn't see that I was just as angry at the traitor as they were.

"It wasn't me," I growled back. "Otherwise I

would still be sitting in that cell. Understand? I'm not the motherfucker you're looking for."

"Like hell you aren't." He grabbed my shirt and started shaking me. Before I could think, my hand was balled into a fist and being directed at his head.

We scuffled as everyone acted as our audience. Jackson managed to get the first punch in, blocking my retaliating one. He split open my lip, the taste of blood flooding my mouth.

His arm was wound back for another as I landed a punch to his jaw. His head recoiled as he staggered a few paces backwards. The crowd started to shout their encouragements, urging Jackson to turn me into a punching bag to satisfy their thirst for blood.

Jackson lunged for me again but I was ready for him this time. I blocked his fist and thrust a punch into his stomach. He groaned, perhaps finally remembering that I was better at this than he was.

The rumble of the crowd was starting to drown out individual voices. I completely forgot about listening for the voice I needed to find while caught up in the rage. All I wanted to do was shut them up so they searched for the real terrorist and left me alone.

Jackson ran at me, his fist managing to collide with my collarbone. I staggered back a few paces before lunging at him. My fist never connected to his head, one voice rung out and stopped me.

"Private Simon, stop!" Jenny shrieked. She was weaving her way through the gathered crowd, her small frame forcing men much bigger than her to step aside.

She stood between Jackson and me, her entire face filled with disappointment and anger. She was a feisty woman, that was for sure. It made me want to take her somewhere private and help get rid of that stress she was holding onto.

"The show's over, everybody. Get back to your meals," she ordered.

Soldiers as hard as nails all obeyed her command.

Fucking hell she was sexy.

My dick was responding quickly, needing her naked body pressed against mine. I had some pent up stress too and sex was always the best way to relieve it.

She glared up at me. "I think you're done here,

Private Simon. You should return to your dorm and have an early night."

If she was naked in my bunk, I would definitely have an early night. My body ached for hers. I was willing to do anything to have some time alone with her. I could then say everything I couldn't in the cells.

"Step away, soldier."

"Can I speak with you, Officer Ramirez?"

Indecision flecked across her gorgeous face before she nodded. She led the way outside while I purposefully ignored the glares of everyone else. I did, however, manage to get a satisfying look at Jackson's new bruises.

We stopped in the hallway outside, empty at this late hour. If men weren't in the mess hall, they were in their dorms and turning in for the night. It was only a few minutes past nine but some missions started in the early hours of the morning to take advantage of the cooler temperatures.

Jenny looked around to make certain we were alone before she spoke. "You can't be doing those kinds of things, Shaun. You should be staying out of trouble after today."

"I wasn't charged, it doesn't matter now. They need to stop treating me like a spy. Otherwise we can't work together out in the field."

"Please stay low." Her eyes were pleading and I was certain there was more she wasn't saying. I couldn't handle her being tortured like this. I'd barely known the woman for more than a week but it was like I'd known her for a lot longer.

Like a lifetime.

"I need to talk to you somewhere else," I said, paranoid we were being watched or listened to. "Meet with me."

Her gaze flickered everywhere before returning to me. "I can't. I'm an investigating officer, I shouldn't even be talking with you now."

"I need to see you. Jenny, please."

She chewed on her bottom lip. "I shouldn't." She was weakening, I wasn't going to stop until I got what I wanted. Surely it wasn't unreasonable now they had dropped the case against me.

"We need to talk," I urged. "I'm sure you've got things to say too."

"Fine. But not tonight. I'll call you to my office tomorrow. We can talk then."

It was all I needed to hear.

CHAPTER THIRTEEN

PRIVATE SIMON

I waited all morning for the call to Jenny's office but it didn't come until that afternoon. We'd just arrived back from our morning mission when the message was relayed to me.

"She's in Atoll's office," the messenger said, turning and leaving before I could ask any more questions.

Having a meeting with Jenny and Atoll wasn't the kind of meeting I was hoping for. We wouldn't be able to talk openly if he was there to listen to everything.

But I had my order and a good soldier followed instructions. So I went straight there without bothering to change from my muddy camouflages.

Atoll's assistant told me to go straight through. I opened the door, bracing myself for whatever happened on the other side. They'd only released me from lockup yesterday, surely they couldn't have changed their mind so quickly?

When I stepped inside the office, it was only Jenny that sat behind the desk. "Good afternoon, Private Simon." She made my cock twitch when she called me by my military name.

"Same to you, Officer Ramirez."

"Please close the door and take a seat."

"I prefer to stand."

"Okay." She stood too, not to be intimidated by my stance. "Major Atoll and his officers are using the meeting room for a strategy discussion. He has kindly allowed me to use his office."

So it *was* just Jenny and me alone in the room. She had stayed true to her word. I should never have doubted her.

"Can we speak freely?" I checked, just to make

sure. In this place, you could never be too careful. There were eyes and ears everywhere. Sometimes where you never expected them to be.

"I believe so, yes," she replied. Her cheeks started to turn a rose color the longer she looked at me. If her thoughts were as dirty as mine, she should have been blushing crimson.

"I'm glad my name was cleared yesterday. You found the rope and knife in the supply closet, right?"

She looked down before she met my eyes again. "Let's not talk about that right now. This is probably the last few moments we're going to have alone. You said you had things to say."

My head was nodding as I started to talk. "You know I'm not a terrorist and had nothing to do with working with the enemy. I need to know you believe that or there is nothing to talk about."

"I believe you." She sighed. "But others are still unconvinced."

"But my name has been cleared."

She took a step closer. "I believe you, that's all that matters right now. Can we please change the subject? There's other things I'd rather be doing right now. Especially with our mouths."

My dick throbbed with the huskiness of her voice. Talking about absolutely anything now seemed unattractive. I didn't want to do anything except take all her clothes off and fuck her hard.

"We can talk about anything you want, dumpling." I watched the smile as it spread over her lips. She was completely different when we were alone. There was no trace of Officer Ramirez and the duty she had to perform. We were only Jenny and Shaun, the strangers who had fucked in an airport restroom.

"I want to talk about your clothes and how to get them off."

I quickly reached out and tugged her closer against me. I grabbed onto her legs, just below her ass, and picked her up. She quietly laughed with surprise. I swung her around a few times, wanting to hear those giggles continue.

When I put her down, the look on her face was nothing short of outrageously happy. The fact we were doing this in Atoll's office made it even more delicious. He thought I was guilty and now I was having the last laugh.

I started on Jenny's buttons. Her uniform was so pristine and perfect, not a wrinkle on them. As good as they looked on her, they would be even better on the floor.

My steady hands took care of every button until there were no more left. I pushed the starched fabric down her shoulders, catching sight of the black bra she wore underneath.

It wasn't standard issue.

No one in the U.S. Military wore a black lace bra.

"You're a very bad officer," I said, shaking my head with disapproval. "Not wearing your standard uniform, that is an issue worthy of a reprimand."

"I'm so sorry, Private. What is my punishment?"

"Take all your clothes off. If you can't wear them properly, then you're not permitted to wear anything. Do it now."

She took a step back so I could really enjoy the show. She undid the zipper of her skirt and slid the material down her body with a wiggle of her hips. Next, she reached back and undid the bra. Her boobs jiggled with every one of her movements.

"Don't forget your panties."

She pretended to pout before she reached down and slid her black panties down her beautiful legs. Her boobs had me mesmerized. If she swung them side to side I would have been hypnotized in seconds.

"Is that everything, Private?"

"Turn around." I motioned my finger in a circle until she moved. "You also need a spanking so you will remember to obey your commands in the future."

"Yes, Private."

I rubbed at the skin on her tight ass, enjoying every moment that I made her wait. She was a sexy girl and liked her punishment. There was no way to keep evidence of her pleasure hidden from me. I knew if I touched her cunt it would already be wet. There was a wild fire inside Officer Jenny Ramirez and I wanted to unleash it.

My hand tapped her bottom and she squirmed. It wasn't from the pain because I'd barely touched her. It was from pure delight. She'd probably never had a man treat her the way I did and reveled in the difference.

"You're a bad little slut, aren't you, Jenny?"

"Yes, Private."

"Remember that when I'm fucking you. Turn around."

She followed the command and turned back to me. It was taking all my self-control not to pull her against me again so I could feel all the curves of her body. I didn't want to rush things, I couldn't let myself jump ahead.

"Should I take my clothes off now?" I asked. I loved watching the way her face changed from placid to fiery in the space of a few seconds. There was a tiger hidden behind her gorgeous façade.

"Yes, I think you should," she said, covering her mouth with her hand so I couldn't see her smile. Little did she realize that was one of her best features.

My cock was already hard and pulsing, I wouldn't be able to wait too much longer before I took her. We probably didn't have that much time either. I needed to take my uniform off, I was way too overdressed for the occasion.

If I knew I was going to be getting naked with

Jenny, I would have showered before the meeting. Peeling off my muddy and sweaty uniform was a relief. I did away with my shirt quickly before doing the same to my pants. My dog tags swung around my neck, resting in the middle of my chest.

My underwear was the last to go and Jenny watched me intently I pulled them down my legs. It was cooler in Atoll's office and so much better than being out in the middle of the desert with bombs exploding and guns constantly firing.

We stepped closer to one another like two magnets coming into each other's force field. My hands slipped around to her back, rubbing the soft skin until she was about to melt for me.

Her hands were somewhere more intimate. She gripped my cock with both of them, her little fingers tightening around my manhood. Pumping her hands up and down my shaft with just enough grip she had me weakening at the knees.

"Dumpling, you keep doing that and this is going to be all over before you're satisfied."

She laughed but I was serious. I gripped both her hands and took them away from my cock. I missed her touch instantly but I was a gentleman, she deserved to get some fun of her own before giving me mine.

I picked her up and placed her on the edge of Atoll's desk, making sure her legs were open for me. I stood between them just to make sure they stayed that way.

Her lips were tasty as I pressed mine onto them. I lapped at her mouth, tugging her bottom lip with my teeth until she moaned. Her neck was just as delicious as I followed the curve with my lips and tongue. I wanted to taste every inch of her but it would have to wait for a time when we could be as slow as we wanted to be.

I cupped her cunt with one hand and held her close against me with the other. My fingers tickled through her folds, finding her just as soaking wet as I expected to. She responded so well to my body that it was like a match made in heaven. Just being in one another's radius was enough to get us as horny as hell.

There was something about Jenny, I'd felt it the moment I saw her in the airport lounge. She sparkled with an effervescence that I'd never seen before. Even in these private moments between us, it was there and shining for me to bask in.

I hoped some of that sparkle would rub off on me one day. Maybe then everyone wouldn't think I was capable of being a traitor like they all did now.

Her head lolled against my shoulder as I stroked her clit. I alternated the pressure, going from soft to hard and watching the reaction on her face. She looked completely content in her pleasure but I was only just getting started.

"You like that, baby?"

She moaned an answer that I took to be approval. Her neck was open to me and just begging to be kissed. I trailed a line down the curve, making sure to tickle in all the right places. She was quickly swept up in all the sensations.

Her hips were undulating against my hand, telling me she was close to coming. I focused on the way her body reacted to each of my movements, rubbing her clit in circles that were both fast and slow.

"Like that," she breathed. "Do it like that."

I liked a woman that knew what she wanted and

wasn't afraid to ask for it.

Two fingers rubbed over her clit, wet with her juices. It was easy to glide through her folds and give her the attention she needed. Her face was both serene and impatient as she fought to control herself. I was doing everything I could so that she lost all that control.

My fingers toyed with her clit, dragging it around and placing pressure on her nub so she had no choice except to go with the rush of joy.

"Come for me, dumpling. Close your eyes and let go," I whispered in her ear.

My cock was bursting at the seams, desperate to plunge into that tight cunt and fuck her as hard as I could. But first, she needed to have her world rocked.

I increased the speed, flicking her clit so she couldn't hold on a moment later. I could see the moment the wave hit her and swept her away. She bit on her bottom lip as her body tensed and then relaxed. She held my hand still over her pussy while her body was overcome with pure bliss.

Her body shook slightly against me, a slight sheen

of sweat making her skin shimmer. She was so fucking gorgeous when she climaxed. I was so lucky to be able to see her in her private moment.

"Shaun," she whispered.

"I'm right here, dumpling. Take all the time you need, but I'm not done with you yet."

We held each other in the sticky heat of the office. Someone really needed to crank up the air conditioning in the small space. I knew Major Atoll liked making recruits sweat but I'm sure this wasn't what he had in mind.

Her hands wrapped around me as she sat up straight again. She pushed her lips onto mine, kissing me deeply and thoroughly. She made my cock throb with need, telling me to take her now and fuck her hard.

I pulled Jenny against me as she wrapped her legs around my waist. I lifted her off the desk and staggered backwards until I was behind the desk. I felt around until I found Atoll's chair and sat down. It creaked under our combined weight.

"Ride me, Jenny," I whispered into her ear. Her legs straddled mine, our genitals dangerously close and oh-so-ready. Just a little shift and I would be inside her. My cock needed to be sheathed in her cunt.

She instantly reacted to my command, repositioning herself until she was hovering over my dick. "Come on, dumpling, you know what I want."

A sexy little smirk quirked her lips, letting me know she knew exactly what she was doing to me. My breathing was ragged with anticipation. My cock felt like it would explode if I didn't shoot my load soon. And she was being a vixen, teasing me with the tightness of her cunt.

My hands went to her boobs, kneading them between my fingers and working her nipples into tight little peaks. She pushed them further into my grasp while she pushed down on my cock. My dick inched into her as her cunt made room for me.

We fit together as if this was exactly how we were supposed to be. I took her boob into my mouth, sucking on her nipple and swirling lazy circles around them with my tongue. There was nothing I loved more than a woman with good tits.

Her hips rolled back and forth, playing with my

cock inside her so it felt good for both of us. My orgasm was building in my balls and rippling through my cock, threatening to come too quickly.

"Touch yourself," I commanded. She stopped completely still for a moment.

"I can't do that in front of you," she replied, her voice sultry.

"I want you to."

She hesitated for a moment more. I didn't want to force her into doing something she didn't want to do but I didn't want her to be embarrassed either. She could do anything and I wouldn't judge her for it.

"I couldn't—"

I took her hand in mine and slid it down her naked body until we reached her pussy. I didn't stop there, guiding her hand into the folds and showing her how I wanted her to touch herself.

"That's it, dumpling. Rub your beautiful pussy, I want to see you do it. Close your eyes."

Her eyelids closed as she continued to toy with her clit. Her hips never stopped moving, my hands on her hips and making sure the rhythm stayed steady. My own hips rocked, bucking against her to make sure she took me in as deep as I could go.

And I went deep.

She buried my cock in her until my balls happily sat against her ass. She continued to touch herself and it was the sexiest thing I had ever seen. She was lost in her own joyous bubble as my lips sucked on her nipple, alternating between them both.

Her cunt was so fucking tight, milking me for everything I was worth. The office chair squeaked, and for a fleeting moment I worried that someone would hear and investigate. We'd both lose our jobs if the major saw what we were doing in his office.

On his chair.

The man had caused me enough grief, it was good to get something back on him. He'd be in here later without the slightest clue of what we had done.

A smirk skipped across my lips.

I nibbled gently on Jenny's nipple, earning a moan from her. She was getting a good workout as she writhed on my cock and massaging her clit. Her pace started to kick up as we barreled toward our peak.

Breath hissed between my lips as my body was overcome with the sudden urge to cum. I needed it, I needed Jenny to move faster so I could reach ecstasy.

I grabbed her hips again. "Faster, baby. Do it faster."

She moved quicker, her hips pumping up and down on my cock as my own body moved with the new urge. Blood pounded through me as my heart tried to keep up. I was chasing the exquisite feeling, determined to get there in the shortest amount of time possible.

Jenny whimpered as her cunt contracted. She beat me to the punchline, which was exactly how it should have been. Her hands stilled and then gripped me tightly. Her fingers were wet from her own juices, I could feel the warmth on my chest under her touch.

A look of complete calm rested on her face. I focused on her sexy eyes as I was washed away with the full force of the orgasm.

My body burned from the fire that spread through me. Swear words fell from my mouth as I was overcome with the feeling. My cock twitched and pumped my seed into her, one burst at a time.

She fell against me and I held her there. Our bodies were completely naked. There was nothing like the feel of skin on skin with the person you loved. It seemed even more intimate than the act of sex.

My heart was still pounding too as the orgasm made its way out of me. It ebbed and flowed like a wave, bringing me the kind of joy that people wrote songs about. It was better than a workout at the gym, more effective that the strongest anti-depressant.

Jenny was my drug.

My cock started to go soft while still inside her. I was so relaxed I couldn't even think to move. If someone walked in now it would be all over for us. The adrenalin in my bloodstream wouldn't let me care about the consequences.

Right now, all I wanted to do was curl up with Jenny and sleep. The rest of the world could wait, it could go fuck itself. All I wanted was to be with her and for nothing else to matter.

"Hmm," she moaned as she pushed up so we could see one another's face. "That was amazing."

I couldn't stop the grin. "You are the amazing one. I didn't know you could get any sexier and then you go, upping the sexiness until it flew off the charts."

She playfully slapped my chest. "I can't help it, *you* made me feel like I can do anything. I completely forgot about being shy."

"Nothing shy about you, dumpling."

She raised her eyebrows at me with a playful smirk on her lips.

Then we froze.

Someone knocked on the door.

CHAPTER FOURTEEN

OFFICER JENNIFER RAMIREZ

All the afterglow I was basking in completely flew out the window with that single insistent knocking on the major's door.

I exchanged a panicked look with Shaun. Alarm was apparent on his face too. Whoever was behind that door, I needed to get rid of them.

Fast.

"Who is it?" I called out. I was certain it sounded like I was up to no good, even with saying just three little words. If one person caught us, the news would flow through the base like a cold.

"Atoll," he barked back.

At least he didn't just barge in, that was something. His door didn't have a working lock on it – I'd checked before taking the risk.

"Give me a moment," I replied.

And then, we moved.

Shaun's cock was still inside me as I lifted off him. Everything felt sticky and wet, evidence of our coupling. The scent of sex seemed to linger in the air, betraying what we had been doing in the small office.

We both moved faster than ever before. I'd never been caught having sex before. I was the cautious type, the girl who locked the door and turned off the lights before any clothes came off. Shaun was a bad influence on me in the best possible way.

Just as long as it didn't cost us our lives or reputations. Shaun might be able to get out of it relatively unscathed, but a female wouldn't. Officers, especially those of my gender, didn't have sex with soldiers and stick around to tell the story. We were named and shamed before being turned out.

Articles of clothing that had been so gently removed were now thrown on with reckless abandonment. My bra strap got caught up, twisting in ways it shouldn't have, but there was no time to do anything about it. I pulled on my blouse and did the buttons up, hoping they were all in the right order.

Shaun stood dressed before me and handed over my skirt so I could slide it on. He looked completely normal, like we'd only just had a regular meeting. I, on the other hand, was certain I looked like I'd just been fucked.

"Ramirez," Major Atoll barked again. He was probably about two seconds away from opening that door. He could come through it any second now.

I smoothed down my hair and silently asked Shaun if I was presentable. He smirked and then gave me a thumbs up. I guessed that would have to do.

We sat down on different sides of the desk and I quickly checked the room. The only signs I could see was the empty edge of the desk. I quickly pushed Major Atoll's things back over to the other side.

Just as the door opened.

"Major Atoll, sorry to keep you. We were just running over a few details," I said, standing. I smoothed my uniform, praying it looked exactly the same as before our sex session.

He walked into the room. "I hope I wasn't interrupting anything."

"No, sir. We were just about finished here, actually."

Shaun stood too as we awkwardly waited around in a triangle. I looked pointedly at him but he didn't catch my hint to leave. If Major Atoll spent too much time with us, I was certain he would know what we'd just been up to.

I knew having sex with Shaun was a bad idea. I knew it was something that would condemn me if discovered. Even knowing all that, I had done it anyway. My hormones had spoken for me and won out over reason. My feelings for Shaun were too much to handle logically.

"Well, then, Private Simon you are free to go," I said, clearing my throat. I needed him to be out of my sight so I could calm down. I needed to act like a normal human being and it felt like I wouldn't be able to do that with him around.

He saluted the major and left, finally I was able to breathe a sigh of relief. I faced my superior. "Major, is there anything I can help you with?"

"Simon's surveillance team said he has been in here with you for the last hour. I hope you found something to support our case?" Atoll didn't have a friendly bone in his body when it came to speaking with me. He was all business since we'd arrested Shaun and then let him go again. I knew he thought I wasn't doing my job well enough, but that was only his opinion. My bosses would understand my position about needing more evidence.

I needed to formulate a lie quickly. "I called him to my office for a meeting. I thought if we discussed who *he* thought was the traitor, he might reveal information he didn't mean to."

"That's why we have a surveillance team on him. He was supposed to be left alone so he could lead us to his Taliban handler. He's not going to do that while he's in here spinning more lies." His voice was raising higher and higher the longer he spoke.

I could imagine Major Atoll made a lot of people very nervous when he spoke with them. I *was* anxious, but more about what was at stake here rather than his disapproval. I had a job to do which was separate from the army's mission. If I didn't do it, I would face consequences from people a lot higher up than him.

"With all due respect, sir—"

"Do your job, officer. I've given you some leeway here, don't choke on the extra slack."

There was an unspoken dismissal in his tone. I knew when it was time to leave. Not just for my sake, but for his, too. I had to bite my tongue so I didn't tell him exactly what I thought about him.

"Good evening, sir." I left before either of us could say another word.

And almost ran straight into Shaun.

One look at him and I knew he had heard every word we had said. He shook his head and then took off. I desperately wanted to chase after him and explain but I couldn't do that with his surveillance team shadowing him. They would know there was something going on between us.

I could have cried out from frustration. No matter which way I turned I was getting into trouble. I never imagined anything like this was going to happen when I left the U.S. for this assignment. It was supposed to be simple, find the traitor. With so many feelings and emotions involved, it was proving to be anything but.

One member of Shaun's surveillance team gave me a nod as he took off after him. I didn't want to be a part of their secret. I didn't believe Shaun needed to be followed and watched, I wouldn't have him thinking anything else.

But he thought I did.

And I couldn't tell him otherwise.

After the intimate and wonderful moment we had just shared, this was the last thing I wanted him to think. Without me being able to explain, he would definitely think I was playing him. Did he think I was having sex with him for answers? Did he think I was as heartless as others made me out to be?

I walked to the mess hall, hoping Shaun would be there so I could discreetly say something. The place was crowded, several missions must have recently been completed and the soldiers all hungry upon returning.

But Shaun was nowhere in sight.

The members of his troop were all eating but he

wasn't with them. He would have been just as hungry, especially after our session in the major's office. I was tempted to wait there for him but it would have been suspicious.

I couldn't go to his dorm because his invisible shadow would see and report back to Major Atoll. All I could really do was go back to my own dorm but there was no way I would be able to sleep in my current state.

The best thing I could do now was to work out who the real traitor was. It would ensure I kept Major Atoll, Shaun, and my bosses happy. Plus, it would save lives by taking him out of the field.

With the command meeting being over, I returned to my old makeshift office and took out everything I had about the case. Somewhere in the base was someone reporting to the Taliban. If I scoured through the information enough, maybe I would be able to find them.

I was surrounded by reports and transcripts of conversations. I had spent hours interviewing people since I arrived and one of them could have been the one I was searching for.

The only thing I knew in my heart was that it wasn't Shaun.

He certainly looked guilty, but if someone *was* framing him, then he would appear that way. Sometimes conspiracy theories were real. They weren't always myths. Working in the U.S. Military, I knew that for sure.

The interviews I conducted raised no other red flags. Everyone suspected Shaun and there were no other people specifically named. The odd person was referred to but it was never more than a fleeting mention.

I pulled out all the reports on the events noted as suspicious. There were several instances where it appeared the Taliban had been expecting the soldiers and had made plans to deal with us on arrival. Each one resulted in deaths, either ours or civilians.

There was a school, a medical clinic, the main city hospital, the marketplace, and a handful of other smaller instances. They could have been heavy coincidences, but it was everyone's opinions that they were so well planned they couldn't have been.

The largest of the incidents was at the hospital. There were many casualties and the whole building had exploded before it could be evacuated. We were lucky there weren't more deaths, really.

I focused in on the hospital, again reading through the incident reports. Nearly everyone on base were called to attend the scene and aid the rescue effort. Those left behind were busy with other vital tasks.

Major Atoll had given me a list of every soldier that was on site that day. He needed it for rollcall to make sure there were no missing soldiers that might need assistance. It listed one hundred and seventy-three people.

Each attending person was required to submit a report on their movements during the incident. The reports were used to fully reconstruct what happened and where things happened.

I started reading through the individual reports. I had already done it twice but I could still have missed something. I was grasping at straws but it seemed that was all I could do now. Major Atoll had put a countdown on my investigation, and the clock never stopped ticking.

It took hours to get through the stack of paperwork. The horror of what they had endured that day reconstructed a scene of terror and evil beyond reproach. It sickened me to read of amputations, people being torn apart in front of others, and terribly ill patients that couldn't get to safety on their own.

I tried to remain impartial, reading the reports with a critical eye instead of a human one. It was the only way to get through them all.

Shaun's report was included in the stack, he detailed his movements up to the fifth floor and how he assisted patients in getting to the stairs so they could be helped down. He continually went back and forth, saving everyone he came upon.

There was nothing outstanding about his report. If anything, it only proved how brave he had acted that day. He, and every other soldier, should have been hailed as heroes.

With the last report being done, I counted them up to make sure none were missing. If there was a soldier that hadn't submitted one, they might be a good place to start looking for another suspect.

There were one hundred and seventy-four reports.

I checked them again.

I checked the list of soldiers again.

There was definitely one more report than there should have been. I started going through the list, taking the corresponding soldier's report from the stack.

I was left with just one: Private Luke Salinger.

His report was brief, with just a few vague sentences about searching the levels to help patients. It was detailed enough to not raise any suspicions, but really lacked substance when analyzed.

Hope was starting to spark in my gut.

I went through the same process with all of the other incidents. Private Luke Salinger was absent from every rollcall list and yet he still submitted a report claiming to be there.

It couldn't have been a coincidence.

I started going through the interviews again, searching for references to Private Salinger. I had found a loose thread and now I needed to unravel it.

My eyelids grew heavy as the late night turned into early morning. I put my head down on the desk for just a moment so I could take a break…

***

I woke up a few hours later, embarrassed to find paperwork stuck to my face. I rubbed at my cheeks, hoping there wasn't any ink imprinted there.

A break was needed. My stomach was rumbling for food and I desperately needed to shower. All my reports were neatly stacked and put away before I crept out of the meeting room.

A shower and then some breakfast. Neither made the nausea in my stomach any better. When I was finished, I couldn't bear going back to the reports straight away. Instead, I searched through the base until I found Corporal William Gate. He was the direct superior of Luke Salinger. If anyone knew him, it would be Gate.

"Corporal, would you have a minute?" I asked, knowing full well he couldn't refuse a meeting with me. Not without a lot of trouble being hurled his way.

He nodded agreement and we stepped into a quiet

corridor. It would have been nice to be somewhere more discreet but we were on a time schedule – both of us.

"I understand Private Luke Salinger is in your troop," I started. Gate nodded. "What is your opinion of him?"

Corporal Gate was the typical army type, brown hair shaven short, muscles that bulked through his uniform, and an expression of perpetual lethalness. "He's a good soldier."

"Have you ever noticed anything a bit odd about him? Maybe something he said without thinking?"

"I can't say I have."

He wasn't making it easy for me. Extracting teeth would have been easier. "Do you know if he was at the scene of the hospital incident?"

He thought for a few moments and I waited eagerly to see if my theory had any credibility at all.

"He wasn't there," Corporal Gate finally said. "He said he wasn't feeling well that day so he was excused for rest time."

"Are you certain?"

"I don't say things I'm not certain about, ma'am."

He glared at me as if I had just insulted him. "If that's everything, I need to get going. I'm late to report."

"Yes, of course. Thank you."

Mr. Chatty, he wasn't.

Helpful, maybe.

As I watched Corporal Gate walk down the corridor, another man caught my eye. Shaun was just passing by. He held my gaze for only a moment before scowling and continuing on. I ached to go to him and explain everything. I wanted to tell him that I believed what he said, that I believed in *him*.

But I couldn't. He wouldn't listen to me and his surveillance team would report the incident back to Major Atoll. The best thing I could do now was find the real traitor and then beg forgiveness from Shaun later on. Surely he would have to understand why I had lied to him.

I pushed the image of his disappointment stricken face out of my mind. I needed to focus and I couldn't do that if I kept replaying the same thing over and over again.

There had to be someone who would know more

about Private Salinger than his superior. I needed someone willing to talk.

One of the people I had interviewed was more open than the others. She had been chatty and one of the few who didn't finger Shaun for the role of traitor. Even better, she was in the same troop as Private Salinger.

I needed to speak with Private Sasha Kincaid.

CHAPTER FIFTEEN

PRIVATE SIMON

I was fucking angry.

My blood was up to boiling point and I felt like I needed to hit everything around me. I needed to cause destruction, vent my anger, do *something* until all the rage was worked out of me.

Normally sex would be able to help me out there but that wasn't going to happen. I could barely even look at Jenny.

Even when I'd seen her in the corridor, I could barely control myself. I wanted to know why she had betrayed me like that. How she could have done what we did, all the while knowing my head was still in the noose as the traitor.

She should have told me.

It was the right thing to do.

Sure, her position said she couldn't, but I wasn't just anyone. We had shared the most intimate of moments together and then I find out she was prosecuting me? I didn't deserve that.

Perhaps I was a nice distraction, one last fuck before we both get sent home. Except when we arrived in the U.S. it would be me going behind bars and she would be free. She would be the one making sure I was court-martialed.

I don't think I could ever forgive her for that. I admired honesty and respect more than anything else and she had betrayed me on both accounts. It was unacceptable and I hated her for it.

It wasn't just anger forcing me on, it was heartbreak too. I thought Jenny was special, I thought she was completely different from all the other women I'd met. I thought we shared something that would transcend just sex.

To be betrayed like that only switched my heart

off. I wouldn't put myself out there again, I wouldn't risk being hurt another time. This was it, Jenny was it, and now there was nothing.

I stormed through the corridors like a bull in a china shop. My surveillance squad could witness whatever they liked. They could run back to Jenny and Atoll and have a field day trying to analyze my movements. Let them think whatever the fuck they wanted to think.

My destination was the mess hall. I was hungry and I needed to do something, something that would make me feel better.

The room was packed with soldiers getting breakfast. The din of nervous energy was everywhere. Voices conversed with one another, some laughing, others speaking in hushed tones. They were all rowdy and ready to get out in the field for the day.

I filled my tray and took the only free table in the middle of the room. A small notepad was in my pocket, along with a pencil. I took them both out and got to work. I ate with one hand and scrawled with the other.

It was my resignation letter.

I was applying to be discharged from the military. I'd had enough. Even before the whole shit storm with the traitor had reared its ugly head, I was ready to go. The longer I served, the more jaded I became.

When I was a teenager, all I wanted to do was serve my country. My lousy, two-bit father told me to 'do something with my life' before he forced me out of the house at sixteen. I'd stayed with various friends for two years and enlisted on my eighteenth birthday.

I once wore my uniform with pride, ready to right all the wrongs with the world. What I had discovered recently was that my rose-colored glasses were starting to fade. I'd seen too much death and destruction for it to serve a purpose anymore. There were no winners in war and I was tired of perpetuating the suffering of so many people.

I wanted to go home and serve my country in different ways. I wanted to help people without the need for bloodshed. Leave that to those who still wore their uniforms like a soldier should.

With all my anger and rage, I couldn't properly

articulate any of this in my request for discharge. I'd never been good at writing and my words all got muddled up. My request ended up sounding like a rant but I couldn't put it any other way.

Jenny would probably have been able to make it beautiful. She was the intelligent type, knowing what to say and when to say it. In everything other than matters relating to me, anyway.

Conversations flowed around me in the noisy mess hall. My breakfast was all gone so I had no further reason to stay there.

I signed my resignation letter.

And stopped.

One voice stood out among all the others. I filtered the others out until I could focus on just the one.

My captor.

The *real* traitor.

I'd memorized his voice so I could find him. It was the only thing getting me through since I'd spent all those hours on the floor of the supply closet. It was where I had fueled my rage to keep me from going crazy.

I stood up and looked around, the voice swimming around me like a fly I couldn't catch. I needed to find its owner, I couldn't let him get away with what he'd done.

People stopped to look at me as I staggered around the mess hall. I needed to match the voice with a mouth that was moving at the same time. I hadn't seen his face in the supply closet, all I had was the voice to identify the fucker.

"You alright, Simon?" one of the soldiers in my troop asked. He was looking at me strangely. I probably looked deranged.

Maybe I was.

For a moment, I doubted whether I had heard the voice at all. I wasn't in the sanest of mental places, maybe my brain was playing tricks on me. Perhaps I was hearing what I wanted to hear instead of reality.

I stood quietly and listened from the middle of the room. A dozen men were all looking at me strangely now. They were all waiting for me to lose my shit, the traitor to get his just desserts. None of them were on my side. They would all be glad to see the back of me, the more public the execution, the better.

The voice drifted to me again.

It was real.

And I saw its owner.

Private Luke Salinger.

I crossed the room in two strides and something snapped within me. The moment I reached the bastard, I lunged for his shirt. I dragged him from his seat so we were both standing.

"What the fuck are you doing?" If there was ever a doubt that I had the right man, it flew out the window. It was him, I was a thousand percent sure now.

My arm recoiled and my hand balled into a fist. I aimed directly at his jaw and hit him with every piece of anger I had.

His head was forced to the side with the blow. If I had my way, I was going to keep punching him until his head was just a bloody stump. He deserved every piece of it for what he'd done to me.

He deserved to die for what he'd done to hundreds of innocent people.

"I'm going to kill you," I growled at him.

Salinger shot out at me, no longer holding

anything back. I blocked his fist with my arm, but wasn't fast enough to stop the blow to my stomach. I doubled over as a wave of nausea rushed over me.

I stood up again, barely noticing the crowd forming around us. Men were voicing their opinions, some wanting us to stop and others wanted us to really get stuck into each other.

None of them mattered, all I could focus on was Salinger. He had caused my life to be a living nightmare these past months and he deserved everything he was getting. I had no mercy for him, not when he hadn't shown any to those poor people caught in the crosshairs.

We went to throw a punch at the same time, Salinger was a split second faster than me. My jaw burst into white hot pain as the blow seared through me. It only made me angrier.

"Shaun, stop!" The female voice made me falter for just a moment. I scanned the crowd in the space of a split second and saw the horrified look on Jenny's face.

I didn't want her to see me like this. This was the animal side of me, the side that could make me go into a room full of people and open fire on the enemy. I didn't see humans then and I wasn't seeing a human now. Jenny couldn't see me like that.

I wasn't that person to her.

I didn't want to be that person any longer.

My arm stopped and I returned it back to my side. I pushed Salinger away and stood frozen solid in the middle of the mess hall. It was suddenly so quiet all I could hear was the beating of my own heart and the ragged breaths of those around me.

Salinger's bloodied lips twisted up into a grin. It was nothing short of evil. I could instantly imagine him conspiring with the Taliban to take us down. He would enjoy being a double agent, he would relish in the idea of getting away with it.

I pointed a shaky finger at him. Everyone in the mess hall would be witness to his downfall. "This man—"

My words were cut off as an ear-shattering loud noise rocketed through the building. Every single person there crouched down and covered their heads with their arms. We knew what an explosion sounded like and we'd just heard a big one.

Chips of plaster started crumbling from the ceiling as all the furniture shook from the impact. The lights flickered before switching off completely. The backup generator should have kicked in after a few seconds but it didn't.

Something was wrong.

We were under attack.

In the flashes of light from the emergency exit signs, I could just make out one figure moving toward me. Salinger kneeled down so his mouth was next to my ear. "I'm going to kill you all," he whispered.

I reached out to grab him but he was too fast. He skipped out of my grasp and ran for the door. I jumped to my feet, ignoring everything else as the room that started to crumble around me.

There was no clear pathway to walk. If there weren't people in my way, it was debris from the explosion. I could only imagine what else was going on throughout the base. There had to be pure chaos beyond the walls.

By the time I'd made it to the door, Salinger was nowhere to be seen. Soldiers in the mess hall started to gather themselves together and start to leave. We were trained to attack anyone that attacked us, they were running into the fight.

I was ready to chase after them.

Until I remembered Jenny.

They all filed past me, each one squinting for any semblance of sight as they moved out. I was going against the tide, moving further into the room to find her.

She was crouched under a table. I crouched down to be beside her. "Jenny, are you okay? Are you hurt in any way?"

Her big black eyes looked up at me, full of fear. "I.. I think so. Are you?"

"I'm fine. We need to get out of here." I held out my hand for her to take. If felt symbolic, asking her to trust me now and with everything I had been accused of. All the anger I felt toward her would have to be placed in a box to open later.

Right now, it was a case of do or die. If we didn't get out of the mess hall, it would only be a matter of time before one of the enemy found us there. We needed to beat them to the punchline.

Jenny finally placed her small hand in mine and I helped her to her feet. She was a little unstable for the first few steps, which was understandable considering another loud explosion rocked the place even further.

She held onto me, gripping my arm for safety. "We're going to get out of here," I reassured her. "I'm not going to let anyone hurt you."

"Promise?"

"I promise, dumpling."

She smiled through her fear and I knew it was time to move out. I wished I had my gun on me, ready to fight any of those fuckers if they got in our way. If they were throwing bombs on us, we were going to retaliate. We wanted no more deaths but we couldn't ignore a fight breaking down our front door.

The only light in the corridor was coming from the exit signs. They cast an eerie red glow on the walls, making it seem like we were stepping into the twilight zone.

Gunshots started to ring out in the distance. I couldn't tell which side was sending them over to the other. All I knew was that I needed to get to my troop and fight alongside my comrades. I might have been ready to resign, but I still knew what my duty was.

The problem was Jenny. I still had to keep her safe; she wasn't accustomed to being in a warzone. Even with the amount of action she'd seen out in the field since she'd been here, it wouldn't prepare her for this kind of attack. This was senseless violence and she didn't need to be anywhere near it.

"I'm going to get you someplace safe and then I'm going to see what's going on. Okay?"

She gripped onto my arm tighter. "I don't want to be separated from you. You can't leave me alone."

"I have to help. You'll be safe, you'll be able to lock the door and nobody will get you." I hoped my words were true. There was only one room that I knew unequivocally could lock.

The supply room.

I'd been desperate to get out of there when I was locked in, but luckily I was smart enough to take note of the lock. It could be secured from inside and out. It was the safest place I could imagine to put her.

Walking through the corridors was like walking

with my eyes closed. Smoke was starting to spread out through the base from whatever was burning nearby. I just prayed it wasn't the building.

I continued forward, relying on my memory of the base only. The layout of every corridor was in my head, I couldn't let myself be confused by everything going on around us. The supply closet was coming up on the right, I could just make out the door.

"We're here," I said, guiding Jenny toward the closet. "This door locks from the inside. I want you to lock it and don't open it again unless I'm on the other side. Got it?"

She allowed me to place her inside but her foot remained in the door. "Please stay with me."

"I've got to fight, it's what I'm here for."

"Shaun, I'm scared."

"Don't be. I'm going to be out there making sure we all go home alive and not in a wooden box. Got it?"

Reluctantly, she nodded.

Closing the door on Jenny was one of the hardest things I had ever done.

But it was time I caught the sons of bitches trying

to take down our military base.

CHAPTER SIXTEEN

PRIVATE SIMON

It felt like I was connected to Jenny with a piece of string. The further I moved away from her, the tighter it became, desperately trying to tug me back so I could be with her.

But I was in this fight to make sure that she, and everyone else on base, was safe. If I cowered away I wouldn't have been able to live with myself. I needed to do this, even if it killed me.

Another explosion boomed in the distance. The Taliban had arrived prepared, I would give them that. At the end of the day, the war came down to who had the biggest guns. I just hoped they ran out of ammunition before we did.

They were prepared for this attack, they had time to plan.

We did not.

One of the walls of the corridor I turned into had been demolished. Piles of bricks and mortar were scattered everywhere, no longer resembling the sturdy wall they once did.

I stepped through it to the outside, the sun and heat hitting me like an anvil. It was easy to forget how hot the desert got when you were inside too much. My uniform started to cling to my skin, a bead of sweat rolling down my back.

"Simon! Get over here!" Rafter called out. He was working with a team of men, loading up the M198 Howitzer to send a rain of terror back to the enemy. I joined them, heaving up the heavy equipment to get it into position.

When it was ready, we moved into formation, well away from the danger zone of the weapon. It could kill a hundred men if given the chance. We kept it inside the base, just in case we had to use it sometime. This was the first instance where we had to.

We crouched down and fired, covering our ears with our hands. Even then, the rumble of death it made when it fired rang in my ears and the ground beneath our feet shook like an earthquake.

A loud explosion punctuated the air. This time, it wasn't on our side. The weapon had hit the target and taken out more than a dozen of their vehicles. Our first major win in this fight.

We all went to reload again while other soldiers were trying desperately to get the Taliban out of the main gate. They were coming in on foot, all geared up in armor they probably stole from us. They were each in the colors of the U.S. Military.

"Every spare man to the gate!" Major Atoll yelled out. It was unusual to see him in combat mode but I guessed he didn't want to go down without a fight.

I looked at Rafter, a silent question whether I could go or not. He nodded and I took off, picking up a gun along the way.

We all formed a line inside the gate, ready for the assault that would come once they broke it down.

Atoll ordered us about with his hand gestures, moving us so we were in the best position possible.

An explosion shattered the solid gate into a million pieces and there was a moment of silence before Atoll gave the order. Our guns destroyed the silence as we shot blindly into the clearing smoke.

The Taliban threw their bodies at us, returning fire as they ran toward us. They led with their guns and held them up with cold eyes looking down the barrels. We picked them off one by one. They might have had the numbers on their side, but we had training and bigger guns on ours.

One of the fuckers threw a live grenade at us. "Grenade!" I shouted as quickly and as loudly as I could. We all ran in the opposite direction, ducking for cover behind anything we could.

I dove for the side of the building, hoping it would withstand the force of the blow that was about to be rained down upon us.

The grenade exploded and took out what remained of my hearing with it. My shoulder stung, hurting like a motherfucker all of a sudden. All I could see was red when I looked down at it. A piece of shrapnel was imbedded in my skin, piercing my uniform.

It wouldn't kill me.

I peeked out from the side of the building. From the dust cloud I could make out some men lying on the ground. They weren't moving, I couldn't see them well enough to know what side they were on.

The base was in complete chaos and it was difficult to tell which side was winning. There seemed to be an endless stream of the Taliban coming for us. No matter how many we took down, another ten took their place.

It was very possible that we weren't going to win there on that day.

I thought of Jenny in the supply closet and prayed she was okay. I didn't think the enemy had breached the inside of our building yet, but with Salinger running around, I couldn't be sure. He wasn't playing for our team anymore; that was for sure.

My gun felt reassuring in my hand but nothing was guaranteed. I continued to fight with the gate team, shooting at anyone that stepped foot on our base.

"Simon, have you seen Rafter?" Private Kincaid asked as she ran toward me. I turned around, ready to point at the other side of the pit but my troop had moved. The worry was written all over her face.

"They were over there before. They might have moved further around the perimeter," I replied. I wished I could help her further but I had a job to do. Rafter would have to look after himself.

"Tell him I'm looking for him if you see him, okay?" I nodded and Kincaid hurried away. I understood why we were not encouraged to date within the army. She and Rafter were tight, they were *engaged*. Of course she would be worried about him at a time like this.

"Fall back, men," Atoll shouted, waving his arms around to make sure everyone understood. We retreated further into the base while the Taliban's grip on our base grew.

We had a very real risk of dying that day.

And all I could think about was Jenny.

CHAPTER SEVENTEEN

OFFICER JENNIFER RAMIREZ

I tried singing to myself, I tried humming, and I tried sticking my fingers into my ears up to the first knuckle. But there was no way to block out the sounds coming from outside.

Shouts.

Screams.

Orders.

Battle cries.

Gunfire.

Explosions.

My heart was pounding in my chest and I was scared that it would break out of my ribcage. I couldn't handle the waiting. The long, stretched out moments where I could imagine the whole building being demolished within a second.

Shaun was out there.

I never got to explain my actions or apologize for lying to him. I might never get to see him again and he would never know how much he meant to me.

How much I loved him.

I hadn't intended on coming on this assignment to give my heart away. It never even crossed my mind. But the thought of losing him now made all the walls in the small room cave in on me.

He told me to stay put; to stay away from the danger until he returned. I wanted to follow his orders but I just couldn't. If we were going to die today, I wanted us to go together – not with me alone in a tiny room filled with toilet paper and him out there fighting for his life.

I pressed my ear up to the door but couldn't hear anything useful on the other side. The lock made a clicking sound when I opened it.

Carefully, like my life depended on it, I edged the door open. There was smoke and dust filling all the space in the corridor, lingering like a hazy cloud both left and right. I covered my mouth with the top of my shirt, hoping it would help enough so I could breathe.

I crouched as low as I could and started moving down the hallway. The noise of gunfire and shouting floated through the space to my ears. It was difficult to tell for sure where it was coming from.

Going outside was my only real option. Smoke was too busy making a home in the building and I didn't want to get trapped under a pile of rubble if the whole thing went down.

Men were running everywhere when I finally found a way out. I couldn't recognize any of them, each one dressed the same and all hurrying around as fast as possible.

It reminded me of the scene at the marketplace when the Taliban had started shooting at us. The ground was perpetually clouded with red dust, the sun was beating down hard, and guns were cracking everywhere.

The war surrounded me.

I needed to find Shaun and know he was okay. He had to be. Our story wasn't supposed to end like this.

Bodies were everywhere. Some were dressed in camouflage, others in traditional tunics. It looked like both sides lost a lot of men.

Each one I passed, I looked at their face and prayed it didn't belong to Shaun. This senseless loss of lives was ridiculous.

I'd seen the Afghani war on television and in news reports. I was a part of the U.S. Military, I had received basic training before moving into my role in the administration of the army.

What I'd seen was nothing like what was surrounding me now. I didn't have anyone censoring the violence, there were no sad newsreaders to introduce a watered down version of the carnage, and editors didn't pick and choose images to show me.

War was horrifying.

To see human beings doing their best to kill the humans on the other side was something of nightmares. It was the terrible fairytales parents told their children as a warning for what could happen if they were bad.

I stood in the middle of it all, my jaw hanging open and my pulse racing. I'd never been more scared in my life before. It wasn't just what I was seeing, it was the cries of pain that infiltrated my ears, the acrid stench of gunfire, and the vibrations of the ground underneath me.

There wasn't a single sense that could ignore what was happening around me. War had a way of making its presence known. It was something that couldn't be ignored.

Everything seemed to happen in slow motion. All the thoughts in my head happened in the space of only a few seconds. I knew I had to run or hide or fight or cry but I couldn't make myself do any of those things.

I saw the soldier in front of me set his jaw in determination before he ran forward and started firing at the men by the base gate. One of the Taliban went flying backwards as bullets shredded his chest and bright red blood sprayed in all directions.

It wasn't on TV, or on video, it was really

happening all around me and there was a very good chance I could be one of the victims engraved on a memorial plate in the next few days.

"Jenny!"

My name jolted me from my daze as it was screamed into the air. Everything snapped back into real time again, no more slow motion.

Shaun rushed at me, his brown eyes startling as they peeked out from below his helmet. His shoulder was drenched in red, a slash cut into his skin underneath and still blooming with the sticky blood.

"What are you doing out here? I told you to wait indoors where it's safer," Shaun yelled over the gunfire. It scared me to see him in this battle mode, his words frantic and his moves crazed.

"I couldn't stay there. Not when you're out here. I want to help," I replied. My voice was cracking with the strain of yelling. Everything was just so *loud*.

"God help me, woman. You are a handful. Take this." He shoved a M16 Assault Rifle into my hands. "Do you know how to shoot?"

"I've been trained." It was part of my compulsory training when I was inducted into the military.

"Good. Shoot at anyone that isn't us. Got it?" He stuck a bullet-proof vest over me before planting a helmet onto my head. He did it up for me, just like a parent would.

"Got it."

"And stay with me."

I would definitely do that. Not being with Shaun while all this was going on would be nerve-wracking. I would rather fight to the end next to my man than sit on my hands and hope he would return to me.

If he was still mine, anyway.

We ran toward one side of the wall that had suffered a lot of damage. Soldiers had been in the middle of sandbagging it when the enemy broke through. They were crouched down behind makeshift barriers, peeking over to fire and then duck back again.

Shaun crouched down next to them and I followed suit. It took every piece of courage I had when the signal was given to return fire. I knelt while my arms rested on the debris and fired the gun repeatedly. There was so much smoke and dust that it was difficult seeing if either side had been successful.

Splinters of wood and concrete flew off our barrier as the Taliban army fired at us in retaliation. The bullets were so close I could feel their power as they shot through the air. We flew back into position on the floor so our heads didn't get picked off.

Corporal Rafter was just a few men down from our position. He had a deep wound to his left cheek. He was going to have a big scar if he survived this, but that was probably the least of his problems.

All the soldiers around me looked weary and tired. They'd been fighting for a couple of hours now and it looked like they couldn't continue on for much longer. Every man we had was out there. We were all fighting to the end now.

We would either win or lose.

There were no other options.

Rafter leaned forward and spoke to his men. "Anyone have any ideas? Because all I've got is going out with a bang."

He was talking about giving up.

That didn't sound like a very good idea.

"There's too many of them. They're attacking

from everywhere," Private Samson replied. Everyone else gave their agreement. I remained quiet, there was nothing for me to do except go with the crowd.

"I'm not letting the fucking Taliban get me," Shaun said through gritted teeth. "Or anyone else." He looked at me and I could tell he was thinking of what they would do when they caught me. I wouldn't be killed straight away, they would surely have their way with me first.

"Retreat to Zone Charlie. There's nothing more we can do here," Corporal Rafter directed. Our makeshift barriers weren't going to last much longer. The Taliban were going to get through the broken fence, we weren't able to close it.

As soon as they dared, the soldiers started to change positions and move further into the base. Apparently Zone Charlie was near the main gate as that's where we all went.

"Keep your head down," Shaun warned me. "Make sure to hide behind anything you can."

"Shaun, your shoulder." Blood was still oozing from his wound, he needed medical treatment.

"It's fine. Be careful." I could read the goodbye in

between the words. He didn't accept that we were going to survive the next round of onslaughts. I wasn't naïve enough to believe otherwise.

We were going to die today. Evil was going to take out all the good the base had been doing. There would be news reports and images of crying families but life would still go on for everyone else. Nobody would ever know the horrors we lived just before our deaths.

"Shaun, I love you," I said quickly. He had to know how I felt before we took our last breaths. "I'm sorry about what happened, but it was a misunderstanding. I never believed the traitor was you. Not for one minute."

"I know," he replied. "And I love you too."

He reached out and linked his hand with mine. At least we were going to go out together. Neither one of us would have to live without the other. Maybe we'd catch up on the other side, where there was no war or death.

"Run!"

I'm not sure who yelled that single word, but everyone followed the direction without question.

CHAPTER EIGHTEEN

PRIVATE SIMON

I held onto Jenny, shielding her with my body and pressing her against the wall. If the fuckers wanted to put a bullet in her, they would have to go through me first. She was shaking against me and I wished everything had been different.

If our plane hadn't been delayed in Chicago, if she wasn't assigned to our base, if I hadn't given her every piece of me, maybe this situation would have been more tolerable. Yet here we were, about to lose to the enemy and hand our lives over to them.

All I wanted to do was protect her. I'd left her in the supply closet so she had a chance to stay safe. But the strong-headed woman hadn't listened. A part of me was glad, because I got to say goodbye.

We were moments away from being overrun. I could see the fear and fatigue in the eyes of my comrades. This was it. We'd all vowed to give up our lives for our country and now it was time to make good on that oath.

My family was going to be pissed.

We would all be called heroes.

Our bodies would probably be burned.

Ashes to ashes.

Dust to dust.

The fire raged in my belly but we all knew the fight was over. It wasn't in our nature to surrender so we weren't going to go down without taking some more with us.

I turned around to face them down, making sure to keep Jenny at my back. We formed a small wall, my comrades fighting beside me. I waited for the fatal bullet to come.

A loud noise started in the distance and seemed to

be approaching. We all spared a second to look around for the source. It quickly registered in my mind what exactly it was.

Dust kicked up everywhere as the constant *whomp whomp* of the helicopter blades cut through the air. My eyes were filled with the red particles of the earth, blurring my vision momentarily.

The helicopter landed in the middle of our vehicle bay. All our trucks and tanks were ensconced in their rightful place, giving the machine plenty of room to land.

It wasn't alone.

More and more helicopters landed around the base, planes flew overhead, all laden with soldiers as they joined our fight.

With the backup came renewed hope. From somewhere deep inside me, I conjured up energy I didn't have only moments ago. We could actually win this now, we had enough soldiers to pull through.

Before I could stop her, Jenny moved from behind me to stand at my side. I had to fight the instincts to protect her and accept that she was another person we needed in the fight.

She was good with a gun, aiming and firing with accuracy that I wouldn't have expected from an officer. We stood shoulder to shoulder, taking down the enemy and fighting on the side of good instead of evil. We would make sure they would regret taking us on that day and make them pay for the lives they had already taken.

The fuckers were pushed back. Instead of fleeing when they realized they were severely outnumbered, they chose to shoot themselves or force our hand to do it for them. They would never let us take them as a prisoner under any circumstances.

They were trying to be martyrs but we wouldn't let them. This would be a story of triumph on the news, it wasn't going to be made into propaganda by the Taliban. We would all make sure of it.

I didn't think Jenny could get any sexier than she already was, but seeing her in combat mode took it to a whole new level.

God, she was hot.

She was also making it difficult to focus so I had to concentrate on *not* looking at her. Otherwise I was going to get myself shot.

We pushed the bastards back until there were no more left to fight. We reclaimed our base and gathered the dead.

We had won the battle.

But the war was far from over. There would be many more fights just like this one.

Roars of cheers sang through the base as Major Atoll declared it over. We all thanked our lucky stars for still being able to stand. There were plenty of wounded amongst us but our death count was still in single digits.

I wanted to cry with relief.

None of us would do that, but we would give a silent prayer for still being alive. We were the lucky ones. If help didn't arrive when it did, our stories would have been very different.

I pulled Jenny away from the crowds and found a quiet corner with her. She was the one person I really needed to talk to right now.

"You need to see a medic," she said.

"I need to say this first," I replied gruffly. "I'm not the traitor and I never was. I'm not responsible for any of this, Salinger is."

"I never believed it was you. Major Atoll was pressing me to make an arrest, he wanted it to be you. I only went along with it so I could have more time to find the real traitor." Her words all tumbled from her mouth like a waterfall.

I believed her.

She wouldn't have fought next to me like she did if she thought anything else.

She wouldn't have come looking for me.

She wouldn't have said she loved me.

"I get it," I replied, finally able to smile for the first time that day. The time for words was over, I leaned down for a kiss, keeping my lips just shy of hers to keep her waiting.

She leaned upwards, unwilling to wait for the kiss. I pressed my lips on hers, kissing her deeply and thoroughly. I didn't even care who saw or what the consequences would be.

We were alive.

We were together.

That was all that mattered. If I'd learned anything being in the military, it was that life was a gift and not a right. It was up to us to live every day fully and to experience everything that really mattered.

Love mattered.

I would kiss her a thousand times over, even if I lost my job. I would never deny her or myself of that simple pleasure.

When we pulled away, I'd never seen Jenny look so beautiful. Her face was smudged with dust, her hair a complete mess, and her eyes watering. She looked like my dream woman. She *was* my dream woman.

"We need to help the others," she whispered. I knew she was right, I just wanted this one moment before getting back to it.

I nodded and we rejoined the others. The celebrations had been short-lived; there was still work to be done. We had wounds to tend, fences to fix, and death to respect.

"Ramirez! Simon!" Atoll barked at us. "My office, now!"

The last thing I wanted to do was get another lecture – or maybe get arrested for a second time. Still, we obeyed the order and followed the major all the way back to what was left of his office.

The window had shattered and lying in a million pieces on the desk and floor. Major Atoll still stood as if nothing was wrong.

Jenny and I still stood side by side, ready to fight another battle. Atoll took a deep breath before starting. "It was hell out there today." We weren't going to argue with that. "The Taliban had a coordinated and thoroughly-planned attack on our base. They could only accomplish what they did today by having information provided by someone in the U.S. Military."

Here we go again. I waited for his accusation to come tumbling out of his mouth. Jenny must have been too. "Sir, we have information about who that soldier is."

Atoll looked at me pointedly. "I know who it is." Those words made me want to punch him in the face. After everything I – *we* went through today, he was still pointing the finger at me.

"Sir, I don't—"

"Silence, Ramirez. I know it wasn't Simon. I am trying to apologize for the accusation." Atoll eyed me carefully. "Private Salinger was killed in the attack today, trying to flee. There were several witnesses to his confession before he was shot. I have officers searching his room now and I expect they'll find physical proof there also. That's the soldier you were going to name, correct?"

"Yes, sir," I said.

"Return to duty, private. No hard feelings, okay?"

It wasn't okay. It was far from *okay,* but I'd already had all the fight ripped from me for one day. There was one more thing I needed to do before I left the office. "Sir, I am tendering my resignation. I wish to apply for a discharge."

"Why on earth would you do that?" he asked. I didn't dare look at Jenny to see her expression.

"Personal reasons, sir."

Atoll eyed me, expecting to draw out an answer but I wasn't going to give it to him. He wasn't going to hear me say that I no longer believed in my duty. A part of me still did, especially after the attack, but not *all* of me. Which made me a liability to my comrades.

"I'll see what I can do," Atoll finally muttered.

Hopefully Jenny would understand too.

CHAPTER NINETEEN

OFFICER JENNIFER RAMIREZ

I couldn't believe what I was hearing.

Shaun was giving up his entire future in just a few words. He was a good soldier, one of the best I've had the privilege of seeing in action. His career could have been long and esteemed. He could have retired one day with a chest full of medals for his service to the country.

He wasn't looking at me when he left. I wasn't sure if that meant he didn't want to speak with me or that he didn't want to tip off Major Atoll to the feelings we shared.

With Shaun, it could have been either.

The major turned his attention to me now we were alone. "I take it you have enough to complete your report?"

"Yes, sir."

"I expect you'll be leaving us now?"

"Yes, I will make the arrangements with my office," I replied formally. It was clear he was ready to have me sent home. Maybe he was embarrassed about being so wrong about Shaun. Perhaps he just didn't like me.

"Then I guess we're done here."

"Yes, sir. I'll make sure you have a copy of my report on your desk by morning."

"Take the night off, Ramirez. We all need a break after today." He looked older than his age, tired and weary.

It had been one hell of a day.

I left the major's office as he slumped on his chair and pulled out a flask of whiskey. He'd earned it out there today, it took a lot of courage doing what he did and leading the base to victory.

Everyone would be sleeping well tonight.

Everyone except me.

It was far easier to type up my report than have to close my eyes and relive the horrors I'd seen. Every quiet moment made them pop back into my memory and replay until I couldn't take it anymore.

A part of me kept hoping that Shaun would drop by my dorm. He would have been a welcome distraction. But the later it grew, the less likely it was going to happen. He wasn't being surveilled any longer, he could have slipped in without being noticed.

But I didn't see him all night.

Or the next day.

***

The day after it was time to leave and I still hadn't seen him anywhere. He was either hiding from me, or his duties were taking him away to other parts of the base. All missions had been cancelled until further notice so he had to be around somewhere.

There was only an hour left before my transport would arrive and take me on the long journey home.

I was going to be taking a helicopter to a bigger base and then catch a plane from there. The whole journey would take more than a couple days.

Home.

The word sounded like a relief on my lips. I couldn't wait to be somewhere familiar and safe. I wanted to snuggle up in my cozy dressing gown and sit in front of the television for a week with nothing but ice cream and chocolate.

Unfortunately, the reality was probably more like I would be assigned a new case straight away and be shipped off somewhere new, destined to live out of a suitcase for the rest of my days.

I did love my job.

I just had to keep remembering that.

Shaun was a loose end that I wasn't ready to leave hanging just yet. I did a lap around the base, trying to find him. There was plenty of activity as the soldiers tended to the repairs around the place. Some of the fences had to be replaced in full while the worst parts of the building had to be demolished and rebuilt.

The Taliban had made an impact on the base, that was for sure. The repairs were probably going to last for a few weeks, setting the missions back too. Nobody back home would be told that, it would be reported that we'd triumphed in an attack.

Propaganda worked on both sides.

I spotted Corporal Rafter with Private Kincaid, tying wire to a fence to patch it up temporarily. "Excuse me, have either of you seen Private Simon?"

Kincaid shrugged but Rafter shook his head. "He's not on my duty anymore, I have no idea where he is."

"Okay, thanks anyway."

They went back to work, moving in perfect harmony together. It was public knowledge on the base that they were together and they seemed happy. It was good that they'd found love in such a desolate place. I'm sure their future would be very interesting, if not exciting.

I continued on around the base until I ran out of time. Shaun wasn't anywhere and it looked like his bunk had been cleaned out.

He'd vanished.

Did he really leave without saying goodbye to me?

I grabbed my things and went to stand out near

the helicopter pad. I didn't want to lose my ride home by being late – even though my stomach was clenched with sadness that I didn't get to see Shaun before leaving.

Time ticked by until the roar of the helicopter drowned out everything else. The dust of the desert kicked up into a whirlwind around me. I doubted I would ever get rid of the taste of the desert, even after going home and repeatedly showering.

The co-pilot jumped out of the vehicle and helped stow my luggage away for the flight. He strapped me into the seat as they prepared to take off again.

So this was it.

Going home.

Without a goodbye.

I focused ahead so that I wouldn't start crying. These soldiers didn't appreciate a blubbering woman as a passenger and I would never cry in front of them out of principle.

"Can I hitch a ride?"

The voice stopped me dead as I tried not to look. Surely I was just imagining things? It couldn't really be him.

Could it?

Shaun jumped into the seat beside me, strapping himself in with no need for assistance. He beamed with a smile that was as bright as the sun.

"What are you doing?" I asked, holding my breath for the answer.

"Going home," Shaun replied. He seemed happier than I'd ever seen him.

I was so happy I could burst. I tried not to let it show. "Where have you been the last few days? I tried to find you." My gaze went to my lap, watching my fingers knot together.

"Atoll had me accompany the one Taliban member we caught to another base for interrogation. He thought it would be good to get me out of the way for a day, lest I start to poison the minds of the other soldiers."

"So you're going home?"

"Yep."

I hesitated, not sure that I would be brave enough to ask the questions I really wanted to. Maybe the things he'd said in battle to me, the declarations of love, were just muttered in the heat of the moment.

Maybe he didn't really love me at all.

We hardly knew each other, really. Perhaps he was glad to be getting rid of me. I was some fun when he needed it and now he could go home to start his new life with no attachments.

It was better sticking to conversation that wasn't so horribly personal.

"So the major gave you a discharge?" I asked, figuring it was far safer than any other topic. Although, we could still talk about the weather, but that was my backup topic.

Shaun still smiled like a fool. "He did. I had a psych evaluation and deemed to be suffering with mild depression and a touch of post-traumatic stress disorder. It was cause enough for a medical discharge."

I guessed if he was suffering those conditions, even mildly, they might have influenced his decision to leave the military.

At the end of the day, it was his decision. Maybe something better was waiting for him back home. I was a big believer in everything happening for a reason. Although, I thought Shaun and I must have been meant to find one another being stuck at the airport together and then both being on base.

Maybe my theory was flawed.

"So what are you going to do when you get home?" Next safe question, the weather still remained up my sleeve.

Thank God for the weather.

It had got me out of a lot of awkward silences.

Shaun stretch, like it wasn't a big deal. "First, I'm going to IHOP because I haven't had a decent breakfast in months. Second, I thought I would visit you."

My eyes snapped to him. "You want to visit me?"

"Of course I do. Our adventure doesn't stop here, dumpling." He put his arm around my shoulder. If we weren't strapped to our seats, I would have leaned in for a real hug.

I'd never have let him go again.

"I don't want it to stop here either," I confessed.

Shaun grinned and it was enough to start my heart fluttering all over again. "Well, let's get this baby home and start a new chapter."

I couldn't agree more.

The helicopter took off and we headed for the sun. Maybe my theory about the way things worked out how they were meant to wasn't so far off the mark after all.

Shaun was right.

Our adventure was only just beginning.

SPECIAL THANKS

First off, I'd like to thank you for reading! I truly hope you enjoyed this story and I look forward to hearing any feedback you have on it by way of review, email, or on my website.

Special thanks goes out to everyone who has been in contact with me about my previous stories. I wouldn't have continued writing if it wasn't for the awesome feedback/reviews from you!

For more of my books, and those written under my cheeky shorts pen name, Kenzie Haven, visit Smutpire.com

33982159R00141

Printed in Great Britain
by Amazon